THE NEW
PEOPLE

BY ALEX JEFFERS

www.mbranepress.com

M-Brane Press
St. Louis, Missouri

Foreword

The fact that Alex Jeffers does not quite yet seem to be a common household name among readers of speculative fiction is a deplorable situation that I mean to do whatever little I can to correct. A writer of fantasy, science fiction and difficult-to-categorize literature, Jeffers has been one of my favorite writers that I have encountered over the last couple of years. He is a storyteller of remarkable imagination, a wordsmith of great talent and an editor's dream of a writer with whom to work on a project.

I first learned of Jeffers when he offered a story for my GLBT science fiction anthology *Things We Are Not* (2009). I accepted "Composition with Barbarian and Animal"—a gorgeous, exotic, enthralling tale—for the book and counted myself lucky to have gotten such a nice item for my first attempt at editing an anthology. After I learned more about Alex Jeffers, I suspected that he was a writer perhaps a bit out of my league at the time (as the very small-time editor I was), and I doubted that I'd have a shot at publishing him again any time soon. But a short while later he surprised me with "Jannicke's Cat" (*M-Brane SF #10*, November 2009). And it was then, while reading this achingly lovely story, that I learned of the singular world of Rahab, an oceanic place with but a few small islands where humans live in interstellar isolation from their cousins on other distant, out-of-reach planets. There befell a situation that resulted in the birth of no more females to the last generation of women on that world. Jannicke, an old woman at the time of the story, is one of the last of her sex, in a soon-to-be all-male world where the very survival of the species may be in peril.

Fast-forward many, many years: Science found a way where nature didn't, and the humans—the men—of Rahab survive and flourish as humans always have, living their lives, dreaming their dreams, marrying and having families. But something else also remained the same as it had always been: most males were still born heterosexually oriented but they would live their lives never knowing a single living woman. This biological, existential conundrum and one possible solution to it are at the core of *The New People*. If, based on what I have just said, you have already formed expectations or made presumptions about what you will find in *The New People,* you are probably wrong. Jeffers surprises throughout both with the details of the story and the way his vividly rendered characters navigate through it.

When Jeffers submitted *The New People* to me over a year ago, I was frankly stunned. Because he submitted it for consideration as a story for the normal run of the *M-Brane SF* magazine, taking me at my word that I had no upper limit on word count. Indeed I do *not* have a firm upper word count limit for the magazine, but a thirty thousand word novella that I suspected would be fantastic (before I'd even read a single word) seemed altogether too much to treat as a normal submission. So, what to do? I had already been chattering on the web about my dream of creating a new book in the old style of the Ace Doubles, but I was still pretty far away from committing to the actual doing of it, and I had no idea what I'd be able to get for its content. But as I started reading *The New People*, I realized that I had one half of my Double in hand already. It was the perfect situation all around: I had one story that would work beautifully for the new book, and it was a story that had long deserved but had never gotten a proper presentation to the public.

As with the story that forms the other half of this book, Jeffers' tale is one stand-alone piece of what we must hope will one day come forth as part of a much larger story. Jeffers says he has in process a work called *A Boy's History of the World*, which will incorporate all of his Rahab stories. This is something that ranks highly on my personal list of Books That I Wish Existed. But for now, I will content myself with the terrific pleasure of being the one to point toward this great open window into that world. Enjoy.

—Christopher Fletcher, Editor, *M-Brane SF*

To Ivri Lider/עברי לידר,

from a distant fan

Maybe Tuesday will be my good news day.

—Gershwin

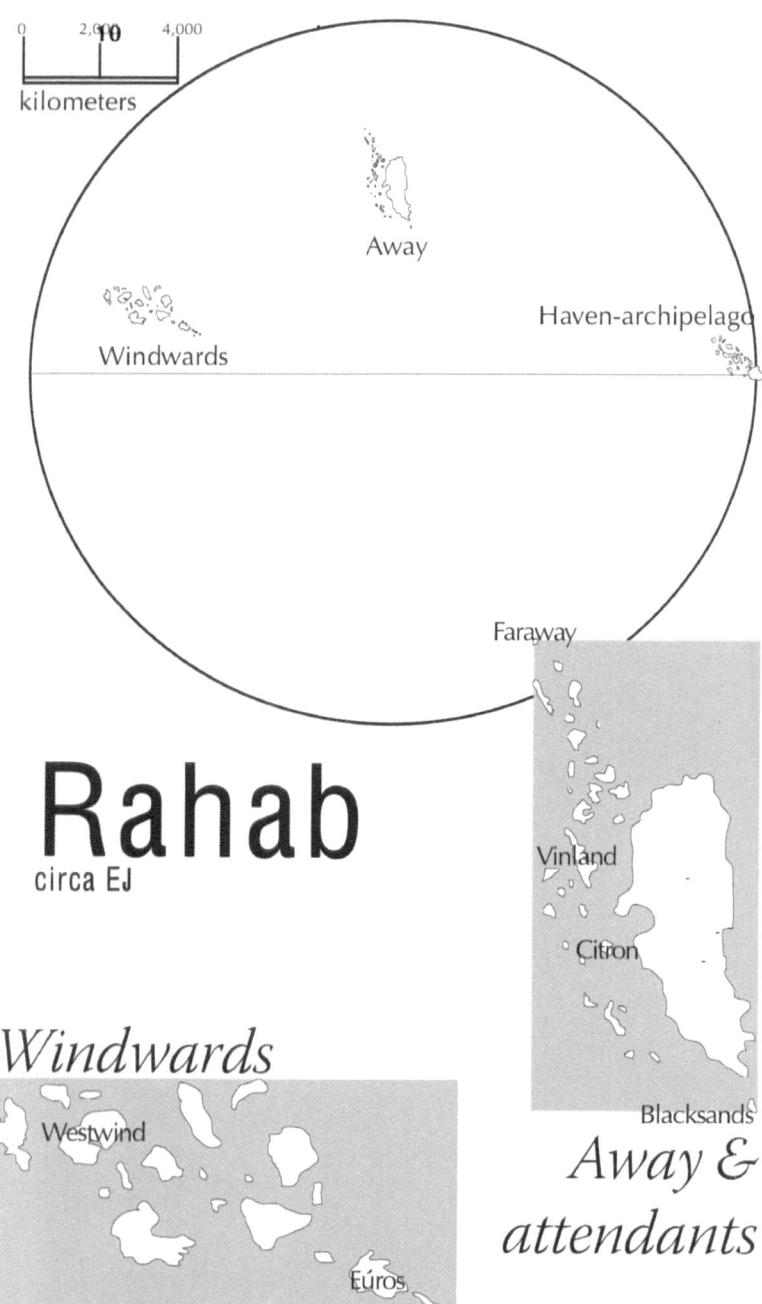

0   2,000 4,000
10

kilometers

Away

Windwards

Haven-archipelago

Faraway

Rahab
circa EJ

Vinland

Citron

Blacksands

Windwards

Westwind

Euros

Away &
attendants

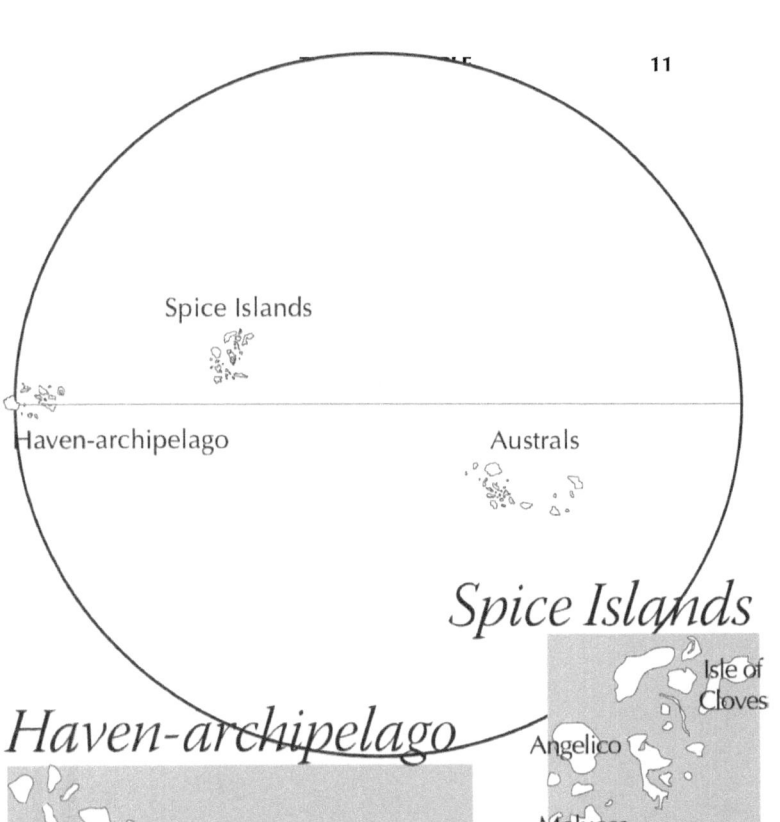

Spice Islands

Haven-archipelago

Australs

Spice Islands

Isle of Cloves

Angelico

Molucca

Haven-archipelago

Haven

Elevator

Praia Dourada

Australs

Terra Australis

Memory

1

Haven-city, Haven-archipelago: EJ 313 Zizdy 03

Running blind, he collided with somebody or something, stumbled, nearly fell, but kept running. The endless clamor in his ears was like surf magnified, roaring. Surely people were screaming, sirens wailing. The phone was out—even if he could have heard anything under the roar—a dead, cold weight on the bone of his jaw. The second time, he couldn't keep his balance. Unseen paving rushed up to strike palms and knees, hard and hot. He rolled onto his shoulder. Something punched his side and he continued rolling until the low seawall stopped him. He kept blinking, trying to see, but there was only light. He felt the inarticulate grunts and moans in his throat but couldn't hear them, couldn't stop them. Pavement shuddered under his cheek as the tower continued to collapse. Shuddering himself, he lay there for what seemed like a very long time, arms crooked around his head, knees pulled up to protect his belly, panting, sobbing.

Eventually the throbs of light in his eyes began to slow and dim, though the dull roar continued in the bones of his skull. When he could distinguish the movements of his fingers, he sat up, leaning against the wall. The fog of brightness made everything hazy and flat. Nobody was running now but he saw people in the eye-burning yellow of Emergency Response moving against the backdrop of indistinct buildings. The façades glowed with a white clamor pierced by prisms of hot glass that made his eyes tear. Unless it was shock, fear, horror that made him cry.

They weren't supposed to have, to use weapons. The *new people*, if that was what they called themselves. The manifesto spoke of reform, of change—not killing. He had wanted to join them, further their aims. They had bombed the nursery.

Pulling himself to his feet, he turned his back on the corniche and its buildings, placed his hands flat on the top of the seawall. Morning sun threatened to blind him again if he looked up. Below, the beach lay deserted, abandoned belongings forlorn on disturbed sands. Waves lapped unconcerned onto the sand, surf burst on the reef. Far across the water, the silvery ribbon of the elevator climbed from the horizon to pierce the zenith, longer than anything, taller than anything—immeasurably taller than the nursery spire before it fell. If he looked right, down the beach, only a little way, there would be débris where the tower had collapsed, broken on the sand. Débris. Bodies. Babies.

Madmen. Only madmen could deliberately kill babies.

Something touched his shoulder. He tried to shrug it off, but it was a hand that grasped hard and forced him to turn. The man in ER yellow was talking to him. "I can't hear you," he said, unsure whether he could be heard himself. "I don't think I'm hurt badly but I can't hear anything except—" The man seemed to be shaking his head. "I can't see very well either."

Wielding some medical implement, the man inspected his ears, then changed the setting to irradiate his eyes. That made him blink, but afterward his vision came clear. Ears remained blocked to any sound but the constant rumbling in his skull of the bomb's aftershocks. The man held up a hand and he understood he was meant to count the fingers: "Three.... Two.... Four.... My name is Jafet. I arrived from Away last night—I'm on vacation. Do you need my ID?"

The man nodded.

Jafet reached for the lozenge on its chain around his neck, suddenly aware he hadn't picked up his satchel when he fled the café. But it was ID the man wanted and he carried that on his person. Tugging it free, he handed it over, scarcely noticed the man slipping it into his journal's aperture. "I'm sorry," he said. "I need to sit down."

Faltering, he reached behind to be sure of the wall and sat. Below the frayed hem of his sarong, ash and dust crusted his legs. There were scratches and streaks of muddy blood—the worst of it from his fall but some might be shrapnel. He lifted his hands: more scratches, more blood, more dirt, on palms and forearms.

Another hand appeared, returning his ID. Jafet took it and looked up. The man's blinding coverall wasn't dirty but creased and crumpled as if he'd pulled it on only a moment ago. His name was stitched across the breast in red, *NISIM*, above the municipal emblem. His face was blank with concern as he searched his pockets. Finding what he needed, he leaned over Jafet with a different tool, pressed it to the muscle and tendon of Jafet's jaw where the phone was bonded to the bone. A thin, angry whine sliced through the roar in Jafet's ears. He winced.

The man, Nisim, inspected his implement, made an adjustment, pressed it against Jafet's jaw again. The whine modulated down to an easy, not unpleasant tone, then cut out. Nisim made another adjustment.

"Can you hear me now?"

Muffled and distorted by the continuing roar, the voice from the aether was nevertheless distinct. "Yes," Jafet said.

"How close were you?"

"In the café."

Nisim's black eyes opened wide. "Judgment! And you got out before the rest of the building fell on you?"

Jafet shook his head. "I told you—I'm from Away. I've been running out of buildings since I could run. It's like an instinct. I hope—"

In turn, Nisim grimaced. "Probably not. We know about typhoons in Haven, but typhoons give you warning, and you run *inside*. The nursery was typhoon proofed."

"How ... how many?"

"Too soon to tell." Biting his lip, Nisim looked away. "Staff, expectant fathers, other visitors: a few hundred, probably. Most of the babies should survive if we can dig the bottles out fast enough. I should—"

Jafet took a breath. "Yes, you *should*. Now. I'll be fine." He took another breath. "Thank you for telling me about the babies."

"The bottles are tough." Nisim almost smiled. "Here." He handed Jafet a foil sachet. "Put this on your scratches after you wash. If the tinnitus hasn't faded by morning, or if anything else feels weird, get yourself to a clinic. My phone knows you now, so I'll check in tomorrow." He nodded, turned away, then looked back, a crooked grin ready to turn to tears. With a start, Jafet comprehended the young man's astonishing beauty. "On behalf of the municipality," Nisim said, "I apologize for your vacation being spoiled." Then, trotting, he was away down the corniche.

What's that supposed to mean, Jafet wanted to say. He was breathing hard again, nearly hyperventilating. He didn't want to watch Nisim reach the ruins—the café where the waiter who'd served him, the cook who'd prepared his breakfast, the other customers must all have been crushed when the nursery behind and above collapsed and fell on them. He hadn't authorized payment for his meal before fleeing. It was the second explosion that blinded him: he had paused for an instant, stupid, not twenty meters from the café doors, looked back, looked up. The slender spire of the nursery—first and largest nursery in the world—was moving, jerkily swaying. He knew it was designed to move, but not like that. At the top of the spire, the titanic sculpture gleamed and flashed as sunlight caught on its facets and curves: stylized father nurturing stylized son.

But then as he watched, the babe in his daddy's arms flared blue-white like a little star, brighter than the sun, searing Jafet's eyes before he could turn and run, before the concussive blast deafened him.

The first explosion had done the job—the second was merely symbol.

Jafet swallowed dry. Madmen. If it were the new people, he wanted nothing to do with them— he wanted them punished, however noble their aims. His hotel was half a kilometer up the corniche, an easy stroll. He started walking.

2

Matxin's Plantation, near Olives, Away: EJ 300 Melky 17

There had never been a nursery on Away. Meat factories, of course, but no baby factories. Away's sons were decanted in the nurseries of the Windwards or Haven-archipelago and their fathers brought them home by sea. Jafet's fathers had sailed him from Westwind to Away in their sleek, two-man sport catamaran, a foolhardy stunt that took two fivers, tacking against the prevailing winds. Fadi often remarked that neither father had got as much as one interval's sleep in twenty between tending the baby and tending the sails. The adventure was worth it, though, he always conceded. Arriving at Olives-port at last, they discovered a quake had knocked half the roof off Matxin's house, so Jafet's first few days on the island were spent in a tent.

In Olives-town, there was a memorial marking the site of the hospice where the last woman in the world died, demented and raving with age and anger, and hundreds of kilometers south, in the mountains where the coffee grew, a monument to the last man born of woman. Late autumn every year, on the anniversary of Jannicke the Last's death, forty or fifty members of an especially devoted god-botherer sect would gather around her memorial and conduct their rites. Many of them trekked south to the Anwar monument afterward, to abase themselves and request forgiveness for the sin of being decanted from bottles. "There's one reason the Ministry won't give us a nursery," Matxin would say, scowling at the postulants as they hiked the right-of-way below Fadi's house. Matxin traced his ancestry directly back to Anwar.

It was the archipelago's tectonic instability and active vulcanism, maintained the Ministry of Births in Haven; its low population and their unusual mobility. Too few fathers would ever request too few babies to justify risking the precious, delicate technology of reproduction. Away-island was the largest landmass on Rahab, nearly as big as all the moon islands put together, crucial to the global economy, but fewer than a hundred thousand men and boys ever lived in Away and its attendants, half or more transient. They were contract workers, farmers and miners, or youthful inductees on their three-year global service, homesick and scared of quakes and needing their hands held.

Fadi had been scared of quakes, he confessed, when the hydrofoil delivered him from the Isle of Cloves at eighteen, a fiver after making his third annual submission to the Ministry of Births' archive. Ready for a story, Jafet sighed and pressed his ear to his father's chest, listening for the steady thump of Fadi's heart. He wouldn't be drafted and sent away from home for nearly three years yet (on his fifteenth birthday, not so many fivers before, he'd made his own first archival submission—jerked off proudly into a little flask for the handsome Ministry guy, who flash-froze the precious, potent fluids and packaged them up for shipment to Haven): the threat was too distant and incomprehensible to frighten him. "But then you met Dad—"

"Don't be a silly romantic." Fadi's voice rumbled under Jafet's ear like a distant temblor as he toyed with his son's hair. "I didn't meet Matx right off—I was assigned to the barleylands. They gave me a furlough. I came to Olives to see the other side of Away. That was when I met your father the first time. I was still scared. Probably unpleasantly arrogant, too. He was pining after a young man who'd refused to leave the Australs. We disliked each other quite a lot."

Jafet sat up, betrayed. He glared at his father. "That's not true."

Fadi smiled, lazy, content. "Of course it is, little love. Of course, dislike is the other face of like: Matx had made an impression. I followed the updates on his advertisement when I went back over the mountains. Eventually—I was growing rice in the Windwards then—we began corresponding and became friendly. But while your dad and I are extremely fond of each other, we were never a legendary passion. You may have noticed we don't sleep in the same house."

"You used to."

"As far as that goes. Matx slept in the hammock out here most nights until we finally decided it made more sense for me to have a house of my own. He snores. And I thrash."

"I've heard you ... making love. The night before last!"

"Yes?" Fadi's tone was mild. "I hope we didn't keep you awake. I expect you've heard us both *making love* with other men on occasion."

Standing up, outraged, Jafet walked away from his father. He gripped the porch rail with both hands, leaning out, looking over the property. Pomegranate trees covered the slope down to the low hill where the olives started. He couldn't see Fadi's house, which was below the crest—Fadi had come up the hill for family dinner, whenever Matxin got home to cook it—but he could see the dim grey-blue crescent of Tanin sinking, the tall cape north across the bay, the cone of Jannickemount on Citron-island west across the strait—the best lemons in the world came from Jannicke's orchards.

"Jaf, little love, I know you know this." Fadi had come to stand beside him, but did not touch. "You've studied biology, history. For the very great majority of us, desire for another man isn't the natural impulse. What we're meant to be drawn to no longer exists. That's not to say I don't enjoy sex, with your father or anybody else, I'm a man, I have a penis and a prostate, but grand passion … it's not in my nature. Or Matxin's. Maybe it is in yours." He sounded wistful. "Maybe you're one of the lucky ones."

What Jafet needed to say disgusted him. "When you jerk off, when you're making love to Dad, you dream about fucking a woman?"

"Judgment, *no*." Fadi went rigid—as far apart as they stood, Jafet felt him stiffen up. "What a perverse suggestion! If I were ever blessed to see a living woman, I'm quite sure I'd run away screaming." He sighed. "Jaf, I am very content with my life, with my husband, with our son. But it would be … *perverse* to imagine I couldn't be happier if I'd been born in a world where the women hadn't all died." He moved his hand along the railing toward Jafet's. "In the end, though, this is the world we have and I am a creature of it. It's a beautiful world, don't you think?"

Jafet edged away. "Not—" He swallowed. "Not if you and Dad and *the very great majority* are living crippled half lives. That's not beautiful at all." Fadi was on the point of putting an arm around his shoulders, giving him a big hug, making it all better. Jafet could feel it coming. "I don't want any dinner after all, Daddy." He pitched away toward the stairs. "Going for a walk. See you later."

"Jafet!"

"I'll be fine." He threw it over his shoulder and started running, dodging thorny pomegranate branches. He didn't begin to cry until he reached the bottom of the hill. Sobbing, he leaned against the trunk of a hundred-year-old olive. He didn't know who he was crying for: Fadi, or Matxin, or himself. Or the whole imperfect, damaged world.

He walked, through the olives, up and over the bluff, keeping well away from Fadi's house. The sun was lowering—outside the bay, Citron looked like a black paper cutout of itself and the silvered surface of the sound was beginning to flame. There was a drop, less than a meter, where bluff hit beach, and the oldest olive tree in the plantation clung to the edge of the little cliff, leaning over the sand at an angle that made the gnarled trunk easy to climb, up and out to a sturdy limb that provided a natural perch for two boys to watch the sunset.

He'd brought a boy here not so long ago, just a few days. It wasn't quite clear whether Yehonatan thought he might be infatuated with Jafet or if it was vice versa. Sitting companionably on the branch, they watched the sun settle and talked, talked, everything and nothing, until Jafet couldn't hold out any longer and kissed his friend.

But was it Yehonatan's *boyness*, the exact, precise quality of his being another boy, that attracted and excited and scared Jafet? Or just the prospect of sex, sex with another person, not his own hand?

Yehonatan hadn't seemed inordinately surprised to be kissed. He kissed Jafet back very satisfactorily. They necked—for a whole interval? More? It felt like more. Yehonatan was shorter than Jafet (who would grow much taller soon enough) but more muscular, stronger. For all the years they'd known each other he'd shaved his head but he hadn't shaved that day and the stubble was perceptible. He exclaimed—with delight?—when he slipped a hand under Jafet's shirt and felt the thick, unruly belly and chest hair that half embarrassed him, half made him feel grown up. Jafet explored the peaks and valleys of Yehonatan's solid back and shoulders, first with his fingers and palms, then lips and tongue. He discovered Yehonatan was ticklish (how was it he'd never known that?) and made him laugh so hard they both fell out of the tree. Landing hard on the sand, they could only cough for several hundredths, before breaking up again in ridiculous laughter.

Was that why they'd stopped? Because they'd made each other look foolish? They said good night without even a friendly hug, though Jafet could see quite clearly that Yehonatan was still as excited as he was, Yehonatan started back up the beach and Jafet climbed the little cliff. He wanted to turn and yell at his friend, but he didn't. By the time he got to bed, in Fadi's house, he felt too depressed to beat off.

He wasn't crying anymore. He wiped his eyes with his shirt, carefully enunciated Yehonatan's name into the aether.

"What?" his friend said after the moment he might have rejected the call. Jafet couldn't tell whether Yehonatan was irritated or pleased.

"Yeho? I'm walking into town to find something stupid to eat and I hoped you might like to join me. And then—Yeho, I really, really want to kiss you again."

3
Haven-city, Haven-archipelago: EJ 313 Zizdy 03

The morning of the bombing, when Jafet left his hotel in search of breakfast, the corniche had been lively with men going to work, boys going to school. Shops on the landward side opened their doors to morning sun: Haven-city faced east, something Jafet found disorienting. For no reason at all, a young man hopped up onto the sea wall and, teetering along with his arms outstretched, sang in a sweet, penetrating tenor about the small surprises and epiphanies encountered in a stroll on Haven's corniche. Halfway through, Jafet belatedly recognized it as one of Evren's recent songs (Evren's voice was stronger, lower—better—and few of his songs translated well to a cappella rendition) but he applauded at the end nevertheless. The youth, embarrassed, ducked his head, jumped down from the wall, and ran ahead of his friends.

Jafet paused beside a pergola twined with unfamiliar blossoms, flame red and gold and orange, each as big as an open hand. On the brilliant sea beyond the reef, fishing boats set their nets. The straight-edged shadow of the elevator sliced across fishing grounds, lagoon, beach— deep into town and across Haven-island, into the west. Fathers and sons and gangs of adolescents and couples in like or love passed him to take the stairs to the beach. On a football pitch whose lines were a matter of faith—the goals were well marked—two raucous elevens chased their ball over rutted sand.

Farther along the corniche, a small municipal gymnasion hung cantilevered over the beach. Huffing, grunting, sweating, admirable, men performed calisthenics, threw free weights around, wrestled. Resisting the urge to strip down and join in (he was hungry), Jafet passed on. He bought juice from a vendor under a sun-colored parasol. As he ambled along, he heard a faint whirring, looked up to see a huge cargo dirigible eclipse faded Ziz, heading north—toward Away, perhaps, though nearly everywhere in the world was north of Haven.

Lowering his gaze from the zenith, he had caught sight of the sculpture atop the nursery spire, offering benediction to the world and all its sons and fathers, and stopped short. He had

always wanted sons, always since he gave up
hoping for his dads to give him a brother. At
eighteen and nineteen, he felt sure he was soon to
marry the man who perfected him and they would
wait only a short while before applying to the
Ministry for their first child. That hadn't worked
out. When he remembered why it hadn't worked
out (he couldn't forget, it was always there
waiting), he despised himself, his cruel stupidity.

Often in the years since, although he hadn't
met another man he wished—in the way that it
hurt not to—to cleave to, he had resolved more
than once (more than once a year) it was selfish to
deny his son life simply because *he* hadn't the will
to choose a husband. The Ministry of Births did
not discriminate against unpartnered applicants,
presuming they met qualifications. His son and he
would never be told the other half of the boy's
genetic inheritance but that was not an argument
against. (It occurred to him, bittersweet, that his
archival submissions might already, anonymous,
have supplied half the chromosomes of sons he
would never know.)

He put it off. At first the image of his son's
embittered, lonely father horrified him (with the
certainty only a young man ever felt, Jafet *knew* he
would never love again), then he feared he
wouldn't meet the Ministry's standards: he was
young, untried—still a draftee serving at the whim
of the induction board. Later, embarking on his
career, he was too busy. His income was
unpredictable. The government's family subsidy
would ensure his child did not want but he wished
his son not to want at all.

Those excuses had long been rendered moot. Stable and prosperous, he lived in a pleasant house outside Olives—not so far at all from his own fathers—could furnish as nearly ideal a childhood as might be imagined. He travelled a good deal, but travel could be delegated or the boy might accompany him. The experience of any number of transactions had been enlivened by the presence of his counterpart's child. Just shy of twenty-eight, now, he watched valued employees younger than himself embark, expectant, hopeful, nervous with good intention, on fatherhood, and knew he could do the same.

He continued to put it off. Love affairs had intervened (if none encompassed what he remembered as love or a man he imagined welcoming into his life as he would a child), minor business crises that he fooled himself into believing major as they were happening, inertia. Always, the knowledge that, if not for long-ago stupidity and fear and stupid pride, he should not be alone. Twice, quixotic, he went so far as to call down from the aether the list of names presently available. Even if he filtered the list—by initial phoneme, say; or by cultural tradition, though then the question became *which* tradition, since his own preferred a boy's name not reflect either parent—there were thousands to choose from: a check in itself.

Always love was in the back of his mind. Not paternal love, for of that he seldom doubted he would have sufficient. The love his own parents wistfully claimed never to have felt, for each other or indeed anybody. He had known love, in so many ways he had been defined by love, there was still so much love in him. It made his heart desolate to remember how small the chance his son would have that capacity, that chance.

At the last parliamentary election, he had attempted to determine the parties' stances on the Ministry of Births, their policies on the manifest unfitness (unfairness) of the Ministry's policies—or was it lack of policy? It seemed there were none. Even the smallest, most oppositional parties had nothing to say. He wrote to the MP who represented the Olives riding at Parliament-island—he had voted for the man—and his three challengers. In short order, he received formal replies thanking him for his interest in the campaigns, none of which acknowledged (still less answered) his query. In the end, he gave his vote to the party he judged least likely to interfere in local business and most likely to spend his taxes wisely. As in the past, that party remained in opposition.

Meanwhile, the inquiry he'd sent into the aether discovered for him an anonymous document that helped him define his own convictions. The New People's Manifesto demanded open debate of the unwritten, unspoken, invisible biases that guided the Ministry of Births. For three centuries government had avoided the issue. Nobody more than they, wrote the New People, regretted the extinction of women, but it was past time to acknowledge Eve's judgment as irreversible. It did the commonwealth no good and the majority of individual men much harm to pretend otherwise. The men of Rahab deserved the right to determine their own happiness and that of their sons. They were owed—not just the random lucky minority but *all men*—the opportunity of passion, of love. It was immoral to obstruct the commonwealth's welfare. An immoral government had no justification.

Jafet could not discover who the New People were but their cause was his. They wished for their unconceived sons what he did for his. He wanted to join them: he wanted to offer them support, if only he could find them.

Although not so difficult to find, the manifesto was protected somehow: could not be copied or downloaded. You might pigeonhole it for your journal or worktable but the pigeonhole expired at unexpected intervals, without warning: you'd look, find it empty. On every access, you were informed no traceable record would be retained.

It seemed to have appeared in the aether *ex nihilo*, uploaded intact via an unregistered, anonymous device. That device had subsequently been purchased and registered by a craftsman of Aíolos in the Windwards, but no evidence suggested a link between him and the manifesto. Jafet's trace, indeed, indicated the manifesto had entered the aether from a very particular time and place: a place half the world away from Aíolos, a public pleasance on Haven-island's northwestern shore that afforded (so the aether showed Jafet) a fine panoramic outlook on Parliament-island—a time, chosen for indisputable symbolism, when the craftsman was reliably located at home in the Windwards: noon, 310 Teldy 34. Jafet knew that date as well as his own or his fathers' birthdays:

five days before the winter solstice, the anniversary of Jannicke the Last's death in 92.

Everything whispered a clandestine operation, a sophisticated conspiracy that wished to be known but not found—not joined. With nothing clearer to guide him, Jafet chose a beach resort in Haven-archipelago for his vacation, planning first to spend several days prowling the capital city and its island. He had been visited by luck before.

So he had come to Haven and the morning after his arrival gone out for breakfast. Afterward, he expected to visit the pleasance that overlooked Parliament-island. He had not found the new people. Perhaps (he feared it) they had found him.

The spire was toppled, the statue rubble on the deserted beach. The corniche, too, was empty of people, save himself, as though a new judgment had come to claim Adam three hundred years after Eve. In Haven, he recalled Nisim saying, hazard drove people indoors. He had reached his hotel. He went in.

In his rooms, Jafet stripped and tossed his ruined clothes aside. He ran tepid water into the tub on the balcony. If he avoided glancing toward the point where the nursery ought to tower or down to the beach and the corniche, if he kept his gaze fixed to the vertical stripe of the elevator rising from blue horizon, he could pretend nothing had changed. The fishing fleet was still busy beyond the reef where waves from unimaginable distances beat themselves to white froth. When the bath had filled, he climbed in, submerged himself as long as he could hold his breath. The healing waters irritated his scratches.

He gave in to a long, mindless fit of trembling. When it passed, he recalled his satchel, lost in the ruins. He would have to replace his journal.

Slowly, as he washed off dust and ash, tension leaked from his body into the water. The moving sun had passed over the hotel and the balcony lay in shadow. The smell of the sea below was similar to the smell of bay and channel at Olives but not the same, as though—if he were to climb down to the beach for a swim—the ocean would taste different. He knew it would be warmer, but it was the same ocean all around the world: it was the world. Even in the most remote interior of Away, one couldn't forget the presence of all-encompassing ocean—even up on Uriel, in the orbital and lunar factories, or the appallingly isolated deep-sky mining installations one could not but recall it. Ocean was Rahab's constant, its context, washing the shores of Away and its attendants and the archipelagos fallen from the sky without prejudice.

He could visit—he had visited—Haven-archipelago, the Windwards, the Australs, the Spice Islands, and everywhere he would find men much like the men of Away—like himself. The language was the same, the essential cultural knowledge and understanding: the foundational trauma that had formed their world. Every one had been conceived of two fathers' sperm, alchemized by the Ministry of Births' geneticists; each was gestated in a bottle, decanted in a nursery, claimed by at least one father. The purposeful nature of procreation, its technological and communal basis, Eve's judgment that made it so, meant the men of Rahab could not ignore or forget the lessons of history. Their own or that of the unforgotten world that had long ago discharged its seed toward the warm, lifeless seas of Rahab. On the ancient, distant homeworld of humanity, with its vast continents and illimitable resources, languages had evolved, cultures diverged, rivalries developed, resentments festered. Above all, reproduction was an individual, accidental, *natural* affair. You could suppose the people in the next valley—in another country or different continent—on a distant world—were not like you, not human as you and yours: you could imagine their eradication without encompassing your own. It was not known but nobody doubted that Eve's judgment was the poisonous fruit of one such imagining.

A possibility more horrifying than the actual destruction of Haven's nursery made Jafet shudder and feel sick. He tapped his phone into the aether to ask the inconceivable question that, surely, he could not be the first to pose.

"Only Haven's," the impersonal, inhuman aetheric voice told him. "The eight other nurseries are being inspected and their security protocols upgraded, but comparison of their diagnostics with Haven's suggests the threat was isolated."

"*Suggests?* Threat from whom?"

"That query cannot presently be answered."

4

Molucca-city and the Isle of Cloves, Spice Islands: EJ 303 fivers 05 through 36

When Jafet turned eighteen and was drafted for global service, the induction board sent him first (it was a half-year assignment) to Molucca in the Spice Islands. For five intervals a day, Rabdy through Teldy, he watched the monitors in a meat factory. It was make work: the factory AI would alert an experienced supervisor of any problem before it informed Jafet. Once he settled at his station, for all he could tell the factory might have been anywhere—Away, Westwind, Haven, one of the deep-sky mines in the débris fields between Leviyatan and Behemot. Not the last: global-service conscripts weren't sent into space. He was fiercely bored, too bored to miss his fathers or friends or home, except for the rare moments when a roving drone's feed took him into one of the tanks, through the simmering nutrient bath, and deep inside the mass of twitching raw flesh. Then fascination warred with unease until unease won out.

Understanding that this conglomeration of muscle fibers and fat, blood vessels and nerve cells, beef or pork or mutton, whichever it was, derived directly from a once autonomous animal was too great, too dizzying a leap—that it was in fact, not so distantly, related to himself. Of course one knew there had been food animals before Eve's judgment, which had struck all mammals impartially—one had seen still and moving images of *cattle*, *swine*, *sheep*, one knew the full scope of the judgment had first been recognized when food and companion animals began littering only male offspring, one had studied the reasoning behind the decision not to attempt preserving those species as men were to be saved. Knowing was not at all similar to believing.

Off shift, he understood the fear his father had suffered at the same period in his life (Fadi's fear; Matxin had never in his son's hearing admitted to any fear at all)—for there were far too many, incomprehensibly many, people outside the cool, placid spaces of the meat factory. Not one of the twenty-three inhabited Spices had a population less than fifteen thousand. More than a million

lived on Molucca, not the largest in land area.
Alone in his small tenth-floor billet (no building
on Away was built as high as three floors) on the
outskirts of Molucca-city, he seemed to feel the
weight of the residents above and below and all
around him.

The disquiet he felt when he ventured out
among them was different. He could distinguish
them as individuals. A stranger might become an
acquaintance, a friend ... a lover. He imagined
Fadi's hope for his son had not been misplaced:
the beauty of men intoxicated Jafet. Grand
passion didn't seem an impossible dream—
inevitable, rather.

For his winter-solstice leave toward the end of
the half-year, he took the intra-archipelago ferry to
visit his grandfather on the Isle of Cloves. Not so
unusually, Lorant had chosen to parent solo, his
sons' second fathers known only to the archive;
unusually, he raised the three serially—Llyr after
Fadi was drafted and left home, Fotios after Llyr.
Jafet had yet to meet Llyr. Fotios was nine when
his eighteen-year-old nephew visited. They found
little to interest one in the other, though the brief
acquaintance did not suffice to persuade Jafet he
shouldn't regret lacking siblings. Lorant seemed
not to appreciate the gulf of years between son
and grandson. Solstice afternoon, he took them to
the theatre but it was an entertainment for
children, intent on pratfall and gaudy spectacle,
that did not enthrall Jafet.

Not the performance but one of the
performers, the romantic lead, an astonishing,
revelatory, magnetic personage. Jafet consulted the

program, surreptitiously queried the aether. The
young man was four years older than he (three
years sixty-seven fivers, precisely)—not an
unbridgeable span. He had joined the troupe as a
global-service draftee and chosen to remain with it
part time when his service ended though he also
performed solo: he was primarily a singer. Several
critics believed he had the potential to become
broadly popular.

At the intermission, when Lorant and Fotios
left the auditorium in search of refreshment, Jafet
remained in his seat and opened his journal. He
navigated to this *Evren*'s aetheric self-
advertisement. The songs that played under the
advertisement—songs of Evren's composition or
choice, each discrete and individual—delighted,
excited, surprised, captivated Jafet. A brief
concert-performance clip and briefer recorded
interview persuaded Jafet that Evren's charisma
was not entirely an artefact of his role in the
entertainment. A gallery of candid and posed
portraits convinced Jafet that Evren's skew beauty
was not a matter of cosmetics and costuming and
Jafet's own distance from the stage. Scores of
effusive messages in the participatory area daunted
him a little, but they were scores, not hundreds,
and Evren's replies were impersonal if friendly.
Then, to odd, somehow antique or alien
accompaniment, Evren began to sing again. The
lyrics—were they words?—were
incomprehensible, but voice and melody were full
of meaning that, in this moment, was intended for
Jafet alone in all the world.

A caption windowed up unrequested. The song

predated man's first venture beyond the home solar system, the ancient language, *Hebrew*, had never been spoken in this world whose name was Hebrew. (He had never thought of *Rahab* as being a word in any language.) A text translation was available, a performance of the translation, several archival recordings from the era of its composition. Jafet dismissed the caption, darkened the journal, listened through three more times, eyes closed, heart—he imagined it was his heart—soaring even as it ached.

When Fotios and Lorant returned to their seats, they might—if they were more observant, if the auditorium had not darkened for the second half—have inquired about the tears in Jafet's eyes.

That night, solstice night, while uncle and grandfather slept, unaware the world had changed, Jafet listened again and again to Evren's interpretation of the ancient song. He never requested the translation, afraid knowing the lyrics' literal meaning might break the spell. Three times he began a missive, each time discarded it. Probing further into Evren's advertisement, he learned that Evren and his band had scheduled a performance Tanndy-night next at a Molucca-city club. Jafet purchased his ticket before second thought could dissuade him.

On the ferry back to Molucca, finally, he composed a missive that did not immediately mortify him. After transmitting it, he tried to forget its existence. He could not—nor did he wish to—forget Evren or his songs.

He went back to his station at the meat factory. It was Rabdy: he had three full days to wait.

Evren's songs on his phone (vibrating through jaw and temples) made the boredom tolerable. In the evening, he went out with acquaintances to a restaurant, then a dance club. Without realizing he had put himself in the way of it, he found himself flirting with, seduced by, a handsome, amiable fellow who suffered in comparison to the image of Evren in Jafet's mind—but did not appear to suffer over much when Jafet broke it off after the one night. The induction board informed him of his next assignment: on Rabdy 41, after his scheduled home leave, he was to report to Bluehouse Mill in the wheatlands of Away, northeast over the Spine from Olives.

On half-thought-through whim, he checked the logs of his own self-advertisement. His dads visited often—it would be peculiar if they didn't—Yehonatan and other friends from Olives, but they checked in, left notices or updates on their own doings, which the logs merely confirmed. The one-nighter man had looked in but not stayed long. What surprised Jafet was a brief, thorough investigation by the bassist in Evren's band, Gerrit, a man who had no cause to take notice of Jafet's existence if Evren hadn't told him. And yet (unless he was peering over Gerrit's shoulder) Evren himself had not ventured—had not replied to Jafet's missive.

Tanndy morning as Jafet readied himself for his shift at the meat factory, the phone informed him he had a message. It hadn't announced a live call two quarters after midnight, so its being a message was deliberate. "You're a sweet boy," the not immediately familiar voice said (he was speaking, not singing, his speaking voice deeper, rougher), "who writes a sweet missive. Gerrit said I should ignore it but then we took a look at your advertisement. Now he's of two minds whether to chase after you himself but he's shy and you didn't write to him. You wrote to me. I'm flattered. Thank you. While it would be a lie to say you're the first to write or not the first I ought to discourage, it would likewise be a lie to say I don't find a great deal about you enormously appealing. I have, it must be said, no inclination to discourage you and every intention of looking out for you at the show tomo—no, tonight already. Tonight, then, Jafet."

5

Haven-city, Haven-archipelago:
EJ 313 Zizdy 03

Jafet's fathers were ... difficult. When would they get over remembering him as their very own baby boy? It was ten, almost eleven years since he had lived under either of their roofs: all his adult life—he *was* an adult, independent, with his own house, his own income. His tax assessment was appreciably higher than his fathers'. Granadas vodkas were marketed worldwide, he had twenty-six permanent employees in the distillery, plans underway to expand again, and bought a quarter of Matxin and Fadi's pomegranates every harvest: their largest single customer. Their initial investment had long since been repaid, while their interest in the concern continued to benefit them. Matxin wanted him to come home right away. Fadi wondered why, with every option the capital had to offer, he'd chosen to eat breakfast in the nursery café.

"It was nearby. The spire is—*was*" (marking that past tense gave him a bad moment) "a landmark. And, you know … perhaps I'd meet an incandescently hot alchemist to bring home to meet my dads."

Matxin grunted. "There's no call for alchemists in this archipelago."

"I'm not wedded to Away," Jafet said, intending the cruelty. He wandered out to the balcony again. He knew it troubled them he hadn't married (Fadi had been all of twenty-two), hadn't offered up grandsons on the altar of familial piety. "Anyway, nothing came of that scheme. If it had—"

"Your incandescent alchemist would be dead." Fadi's tone was flat. "In all likelihood. Three hundred seventeen bodies so far. Four survivors—not counting you."

"Jaf," said Matxin. "Weren't you a fan of Evren before anybody knew his songs?"

Jafet's heart thumped, stilled. He still listened to the music, bought the recordings when they were released, read the press, although he attempted not to leave traces that might encourage Evren (or himself) to believe he was followed. He almost felt he had succeeded in not thinking of the singer as a man for years. Nine years. "What about Evren?"

"He was—he's the only victim whose name has been released."

Apparently his success was fraudulent. The sharp, physical pain made Jafet clutch the balcony rail.

"*Survivor*," said Fadi, who was privy to more of their son's secrets. "He's expected to pull through."

"That's good." The steadiness of his voice shocked Jafet, but the subject needed to be changed, or his fathers needed to stop talking and let him get on with it. He wouldn't give Fadi the satisfaction. "Look, Dads, nobody could have anticipated the bombing. Unlike the three hundred twenty-one other *victims*, I'm fine. I'd like to try enjoying the rest of my vacation. Please? I have a very costly reservation on Praia Dourada starting Melky. I'll be back Rabdy 06, as planned. You can baby me then if you still feel the need."

"Brat," said Fadi.

"Jaf?" Matxin said. "We're not used to you being away from home for your birthday. Check in with us often? You can't ask us not to worry— you're the only son we've got."

One, Jafet wanted to say—don't try to make me feel responsible for *your* decisions. Two—"I'd be more worried about a big quake where you are. Grand syzygy coming up before I get home, remember—my birthday, isn't it?—and you'd better check in with me. I'll see you soon and talk to you again sooner. Fine? Love you both."

Finally disengaged, Jafet released his grip on the rail. White and livid pink marks scarred his palms. *Evren*, he said to the hollow in his mind, hating himself again. Evren. He stared downward over the rail, blank. There were people: life, tentative, was returning to the scarred corniche. Life. The business of life. He pronounced the name of his stillmaster.

"Boss?" said Enric after a moment. "You've barely been gone two days!"

"Heard the news from Haven, Enric?"

"Yes, of course. Mother of—"

"I was in it. I thought you should know before rumors start flying."

"Sorry, *what*?"

"I was in the café below the spire. The bomb went off. I got out before the tower fell in on me. Quake reflexes. I'm fine, but Haven ER knows me so I imagine I'll be on the official list of survivors. So I thought you should know."

"Mother of the next world!"

"Enric, my dear, you know I'm uncomfortable with that kind of language. Your personal beliefs are your own affair, but I'd rather not know."

"Sorry. Heat of the moment. Sorry, boss. Jafet—" Enric had been Jafet's boss, once—"I'm not a god botherer, despite my family. You know that, right? It's just habit. First thing I heard about the bombing, I thought: It was them."

Jafet blinked. The new people had been on his mind—he hadn't considered god botherers.

"They're the only ones would kill babies."

Jafet had never had much to do with god botherers. They didn't call themselves that, he supposed—it wouldn't be *bothering* in their eyes—but he didn't know what the polite term would be, didn't want to ask Enric. He supposed they were just men, discontented, unhappy as any others, who had discovered their own justification for their unhappiness. Could you begrudge them that?

They believed Eve's judgment (it was their term, though everybody used it) was punishment. God's punishment on a world that had been founded in error. The AI seedship Uriel, bringing human gametes to Rahab instead of naturally born persons (who would have died many times over on the interminable voyage, and died again waiting for the planet to be made ready for them—how the god botherers worked around those questions Jafet couldn't imagine), then mixing up people in bottles when the world was ready to be settled— Uriel and its builders on the homeworld had usurped god's prerogative. Eve's judgment was god's punishment for that transgression but it wasn't just the women who were meant to die. But the men of Rahab (and the doomed women who aided them) resisted human extinction, half outwitted the judgment. They spat in god's face.

A true believer, as far as Jafet understood it, would resist engaging with the bottle-damned world in preparation for the next, the actualized world that respected god's plan. He would refrain from unfruitful sex. He would not give in to the urge to bring an unnatural child (unnatural, ungodly like himself) into the world.

Enric's family gave evidence not every god botherer could follow through. They would have died out long ago.

"Rico," Jafet said slowly. "I'm quite convinced your family wasn't involved."

"You don't know my brothers, love. Seoc's in

Haven, last I knew. He gets caught, accused, goes on trial, I'll be first to witness to his bad character. Jaf—you're really all right?"

They'd been lovers, too, for a fiver or so, long ago in Faraway. "Shaken," Jafet admitted. "I'll need that vacation more than ever, I suppose."

"Get out of the city. Beach, drink, drugs, a little recreational sex—I'll take care of the business for you … in anticipation of my own vacation."

"That's still the plan." Jafet blinked again. The god botherers were bothering him. "Enric, you're just a couple years short of forty. Why haven't you settled down and made a baby or two?"

"What was that about personal beliefs being my own affair, boss?" Enric laughed, uncomfortable. "I don't think that has anything to do with it, Jafet. Not consciously, certainly. And, you know, my dads are devout like stout, all four of 'em, but they married up and got their six little bottle-damned botherers and one heathen—I've got a couple of nephews I know about, too. I know for a fact neither dads nor big brothers are chaste, whatever they profess. Were, anyway, back when I paid attention. Me—I'm a romantic. I haven't met the guy I'd want to share the responsibility of kids with. And then I've got this job I love that doesn't leave me a lot of free time to raise a boy by myself if I wanted to."

Hurt, Jafet said, "I'd give you the time, Rico. You know I would. I'd *make* you take it."

Enric laughed again. "As I said, *boss*, I love my job. Anyway, what about you? Fadi's aching for grandkids."

"I'm—I guess I'm like you. Haven't found the

right guy." (Drove him away. Stupid. Hateful. Afraid.)

"You were the closest, you know."

"Wait—what?"

"I didn't take your offer because I expected Granadas to be a big success, Jaf. Turns out I was wrong about that, but still. I *liked* you, love. I think we two fit really well in a whole lot of ways. Only I wasn't in love with you and you weren't going to fall in love with me. So. But, honestly? You ever give up hope of finding the man makes you burn hot, I'd be honored to be your husband and bring up a couple of boys with you. Long as I keep my job."

"Oh." That was too close. All in an instant, Jafet saw three little boys in graduated sizes, running back and forth between their daddies' houses, bang bang bang, wreaking innocent havoc at the distillery, himself and Enric watching over them fondly ... arm's length from each other. "Oh, Rico."

"Drop the knife, boss. It wasn't a proposal. I'm not quite ready to abandon my own burning-man dreams myself yet. Where I'm going to find him on this forsaken island, though—"

"That's—" The horrifying vision vanished, though Jafet knew it hadn't gone far. "That's what vacations are for."

"Good luck with that, then, boss."

"Enric, I ... I adore you. I depend on you."

"Don't I know it. Tell you what, Jaf. You come home, you're not burning up with love everlasting for somebody else, we'll have a nice dinner together and then some happy, no-consequences fucking before *I* take off. It's been too long since we did that. I can make you shout out loud, you know that. Deal?"

"I can make *you* squeal. Deal."

"'Bye, boss. I'll tell the guys you're all right. I'll check in after syzygy. Enjoy the beach ... enjoy your birthday."

Disengaged, Jafet saw the vision again, out of the corner of his eye. It didn't look so horrifying now, somehow, but he wasn't ready to embrace it, or Enric. He wasn't ready to give in to *Fadi's* bleak vision. The sea was blue, the sky was blue—he had survived.

...Evren had survived. Breathing shallowly, he re-entered the room, looking to find his journal. Remembered he had only auditory access to the aether until he replaced it. For now, using the phone, he petitioned the aether for a status report on his old acquaintance Evren.

"Evren was caught in a fire," the voice said without emotion, "resulting from this morning's terrorist incident, on the third floor of the Haven nursery. He is presently in the burn unit of Haven Central. Despite the severity of his injuries, prognosis for full recovery is good. His husband and newly decanted son, however, I am sorry to report, did not survive."

6
Molucca-city, Spice Islands:
EJ 303 Tanndy/Teldy 36

Across the front of the stage, the speedy montage—portraits of Evren, images of singer and band performing, rehearsing, goofing off—slowed as the house music faded. A deliberate bass thumping troubled the final image, rippling it up and down. Jafet recalled Gerrit's visit to his advertisement, swallowed, gripped his sweating glass, settled his weight. Although the club was hardly full, the audience had crowded toward the stage, surrounded him: sweating, breathing, waiting. Around the periphery of the cavernous space, lamps dimmed or cycled from blue-white to red-orange.

Replacing handsome, smirking Evren, a

panoramic animation of spinning Rahab from near orbit appeared. But it was Rahab of long ago, five, six hundred years: there was Uriel floating free, the great seedship not yet anchored to the planet by the elevator's taut tether. Despite cloud and weather systems, the blue surface of the globe appeared oddly blank: *there* was Away-island in the northern hemisphere but it looked small and lonely, unformed, without the chains and flotillas of its future attendants off the western shore. No other land broke the surface of Rahab's ocean. There were the three moons, Tanin and Ziz and Teli dancing their ponderous rounds ... no, there were *four* moons. The swollen globe of Beliyal wallowed around the planetary curve. No human person had ever seen Beliyal.

The image trembled, spurts of bright color racing up the scrim as intricate, repetitive guitar plucking played against the bass rhythm. Overhead, devices like flowers opened to release a pollen of glittering motes that formed a cloud above the audience. Plucking and thumping became more distinct as tiny speakers captured their feeds. Suddenly, intense, blinding light erupted within Beliyal as the shaped charges Uriel's agents had planted blew, and suddenly the panorama wasn't at the front of the stage, obscuring it, but behind. Burning through Rahab's atmosphere, titanic fragments of the broken moon fell. Steam whitened the globe when the moon's islands planted themselves in the seabed, silhouetted immobile drummer and his kit, the two guitarists, bassist, keyboard player. Somebody in the audience shouted Evren's name.

Second guitar chimed. Building on Gerrit's bass, Pherick began to tap his skins and stroke his cymbals. All around Jafet, people caught the rhythm in shoulders and necks, swayed, rocked, but Jafet remained still. Where was Evren? The intro was building, complicating. Two voices, a pair of tenors crooning at cross purposes without words or consonants: Gerrit and left-hand guitarist, Diogo, still no more than black silhouettes but Jafet knew their names, their voices: the arrangement was punched up for live performance, drawn out, but he knew the song. Any moment now.

Somebody seemed to stumble against him from behind, startling him into nearly dropping his glass. Two strong hands gripped his shoulders, a wet mouth pressed a kiss to his neck below the ear, the voice he anticipated singing muttered gruffly, "You're no disappointment, Jafet," and Evren pushed past him. Reaching the stage, Evren vaulted up, turned to face his audience. As the image behind the stage faded to abstraction, a spotlight caught him, illuminated a private smile, before he turned on, raised his hands, bellowed, "It's a *good day*!" and began to sing. His band piled in behind him. Jafet murmured, "Evren?" surprised but not surprised as the beat grabbed him—he was hardly the only one dancing.

Evren kept them dancing. The first six songs were all fast and loud. However complex the instrumentation over top, however intricate lyric or melody, Gerrit's bass rhythms and Pherick's drumming never let the audience go. "Striped Shirt" followed "Good Day," succeeded by

"When You're Alone".... Evren danced with the audience, bouncing across the stage, reeling them on. When Anand commenced an anthemic solo, Evren challenged him with his own imaginary guitar. During a passage marked by the insistent rhythm of a hard fuck, he made out with Gerrit, enthusiastic, theatrical—the bassist never dropped his beat. Another song, he stepped up behind Diogo, mimed humping the diminutive guitarist, who responded with a wide, happy grin. Jumpy with images cued to the band's rhythms and Evren's lyrics, the stage backdrop expanded smoothly until the club had become a 360-degree cyclorama, leaping like open flames in the corners of your eyes.

The sixth song faded out—it was new, Jafet didn't know the title yet—into prolonged applause. It seemed the audience had doubled. Evren stood at the front of the stage, legs spread wide, arms up, head back. Someone off-stage tossed him a bottle. He caught it handily, pulled off the cap, drank. Jafet thought he heard Evren swallow. He sipped his own drink, the vodka harsh and flavorless.

Diogo and Anand were picking away at seeming random. Evren turned to set his bottle on the drum platform. He pulled the striped shirt over his head, wiped his face and chest with it, tossed it aside. "Another new one," he told the audience, conversational. "First time we're playing it for real people—I only worked out the words the other day." Ambling to the front of the stage, he hiked up the skirts of his sarong and crouched, peering into the crowd, then dropped his legs over

and sat. Behind him Branko pulled a low cascade
of harsh, industrial noise from his keys. Cymbals
shivered. "For Jafet," said Evren distinctly, and
beckoned. "Jafet—c'mere."

Startled less by surprise than inevitability, by
unspeakable hope, nervous but agreeable, Jafet
stumbled forward. Behind Evren, Branko began a
simple piano ostinato. A few scattered claps
slapped the air behind Jafet. Evren beckoned
again, till Jafet stood between his knees, looking
up. Grinning, Evren plucked the glass from his
hand and took a gulp. "Yow!" Evren yelped,
making a comic grimace, and set the glass down
safe beside him. Placing his hands on Jafet's jaw
and tipping up his chin, he leaned to kiss him
sweetly. The rest of the band was following
Branko's lead. The applause from the audience
faltered. Jafet's face was hot—he wanted more.
Much more.

Evren spun him so he faced the crowd he
couldn't see, the crowd he'd been one of a
moment ago. He leaned back in the embrace of
Evren's thighs, wanting more. Evren wrapped his
arms companionably around Jafet's neck, rocked
him to the beat, sang over his head.

It wasn't a love song, not really. Was it? Branko
kept the ostinato figure spinning with tiny
variations, sometimes handed it off to bass or
acoustic guitar for a few measures, or jinked mid-
phrase from piano to hollow marimba. The
rhythm was gentle, the melody simple as a lullaby.
Evren sang intimately, warm baritone throbbing in
the vault of Jafet's skull.

A young man wandered the world's ocean,

aimless. He had completed his period of draft labor but not chosen a career—where or how to live. He wanted truth and love and beauty, didn't know whether he'd recognize them if he found them. His little boat carried him to a solitary island that had never been settled, far from travelled sea roads. Alone but not lonely, he built a house to shelter himself, taught himself to live off the bounty of the island and its lagoon. It was just the piano and simple percussion now. Years passed unmarked. There were truth and beauty in his simple life. Massed strings picked up the melody, guitars ornamented piano's ground bass, percussion grew more complex, and Evren sang louder, his voice huskier, passionate. The pressure of his forearms on Jafet's neck increased. An east wind rose. The young man (was he still so young?) saw a simple white sail on the black horizon, drifting toward him in the mingled light of three moons.

Truth and love and beauty.

Evren rested his cheek on the crown of Jafet's head while the applause mounted, bare chest hot, heaving on Jafet's shoulders. Jafet was afraid now, in the eyes of all these clapping strangers, the embrace of this stranger, if the song was really for him. "What shall we play now?" Evren asked so only he would hear.

Jafet hesitated. "'Bo'...?" He didn't know what the title signified—Evren and his band surely did, there would be men in the audience who had listened to or read the translation.

"No. That's always the last song." Evren turned Jafet about again. He was smiling, brown eyes gleaming. "I have to entertain these people, little man—" (Jafet knew he was almost fifteen centimeters taller than Evren)—"though I think I should like to entertain you alone just now." He laughed, kissed Jafet's brow, pushed him away. "Don't forget your drink."

Dumb, Jafet stood where he was. Evren hauled his feet onto the stage, stood. He signaled the band, then turned to the audience, Jafet apparently forgotten. "Long ago," he told them, "when I was teaching myself to sing and write songs, I went prowling through Uriel's library. There are treasures there! I learned so much! My greatest teacher, no question, was a man who died on another world decades before our ancestral gametes set out for Melek and Rahab, a singer who was tremendously popular in his own little country, among people who spoke his obscure little language—otherwise almost completely unknown. Some of the songs you've heard and will hear tonight were titled after songs he wrote and recorded—not imitations, precisely, *my* songs, but homages. We've recorded a song that became his anthem, although he didn't write it. We'll give you that one later. This is one he did write." He raised his arms—"*Ha'anashim Ha'chadashim*—'The New People'!"—dropped them.

Jafet grabbed his glass, scuttled back an appropriate distance from the stage. People made room for him. The bass line was tricky, jittery, doubled by fast, frantic drums and an oddly hollow, syncopated, buzzing drone from one of Branko's keyboards. Evren bounced, bopped, wheeled his arms, as Anand and Diogo added a few bars of high, fast, jangly picking, one guitar perceptibly out of synch with the other. It got under Jafet's skin, made him anxious, excited. Guitars dropped out. Evren's voice took over the melody, talk-singing incomprehensible syllables in precise time to Gerrit's bass. Without warning, leaving the bouncing crowd in disarray, static, echoey guitar and keyboard chords announced a chorus. Evren's voice soared into tenor and falsetto, exalted—unintelligible. Confused, Jafet noted the blank expressions of some of the men near him: understood the aether was translating for them, didn't care to follow the example. He gave himself up to the exhilaration of bass, drone, guitars followed by jumpy, distorted voice, by yearning chorus—by sudden crashing, disorienting silence—by applause, bewildered but loud.

The songs that came after he knew, old friends already, understood the lyrics, sang along (under his breath, he knew he couldn't carry a tune) with the choruses. Some were fast and made him dance. To others, gentle or melancholy or thoughtful, he simply swayed. There was, he realized, had been since Evren sent him back to the floor, a bubble of isolation around him—he was never crowded or jostled: they thought him special, marked out. It made him *feel* special: scared.

"'Bo,'" Evren announced, the single, simple syllable. Always the last song.

"*Bo*," Jafet asked the aether, "translation from Hebrew. Just the title—I don't want the lyrics."

"*Let's* is the title's traditional translation," the aether told him. "Some interpretations in languages other than Hebrew have been entitled *Your Soul.* Literally, *Come.*"

7

Haven-city, Haven-archipelago: EJ 313 Zizdy 03

The hotel's concierge recommended a restaurant, gave directions to a general store several blocks inland. Jafet compared journals. There was frustratingly little to distinguish them in terms of features, it was all aesthetics. "Call from Nisim," his phone announced. He set the two journals back on the shelf.

"Nisim?"

"Jafet. I wanted to check how you were doing."

"I'm ... all right. Physically. I think."

"The tinnitus?"

"It's gone. I'm not even sure when I stopped

noticing it. An interval or two ago, anyway."

"That's good." Nisim sighed. "That's … good."

Jafet took a breath, recalling the young man's professional, impersonal kindness—recalling Nisim's immaculate beauty. It was none of his affair. "My friend, *you* don't sound so good."

"They sent me away! I was pawing through the rubble, finding babies in their bottles, getting them out and umbilicalled up so they'd have a chance to survive—and they sent me away. There's still more babies in there!"

"New shift," said Jafet, trying to sound dispassionate. "You were exhausting yourself. Wouldn't do you or the rescue effort any favors if you injured yourself. Yes?"

Nisim grunted. "I understand *why* they sent me away."

"Nisim." Jafet paused. "I'm just on my way to dinner. Join me?"

"What? Why?" He made a sound between cough and laugh. "—Where?"

Jafet named the restaurant.

"You don't want to go there. Overpriced tourist food." He made the sound again.

"You decide, then."

Nisim didn't hesitate. "Yvo," he said. "It looks like a dive but the food's surprisingly good—" a moment's silence as he checked—"and you're not far. It'll take me maybe a quarter if the street rail co-operates."

"Fine. No hurry. I'll watch for you—though I don't know if I'll recognize you out of ER yellow."

"They know me at Yvo." Nisim was distracted. "Jafet ... thank you."

"I don't really know anybody in Haven. I'd be eating overpriced tourist food all on my lonesome."

Still preoccupied. "Give me a quarter." Nisim disengaged.

Jafet looked at the two journals again. They were the same: one bound in treated fish skin, charcoal grey—the other wine-colored, tank-grown hide. They were the same. He authorized payment for the grey one, left the store.

Cities, proper cities, hadn't scared him for a good many years but he wasn't familiar with Haven, he'd only previously visited on business— debarked at the passenger port south of Parliament-island, street rail to the junction closest to his hotel. All the men he had to deal with had their offices on the corniche. He hadn't ventured far off the seaside avenue before. Streets perpendicular to the corniche were narrow, to funnel the prevailing sea breeze inland, shaded by monomolecular-film awnings that became translucent at dusk. Between tall white buildings, pocket parks and gardens laid with bright flowers and fountains provided pleasant spaces for residents to gather. They were gathering. A wound had been torn in the city's heart, but it was a great city, *the* great city, and life went on.

He asked the aether to guide him to Yvo, turn by turn: inland, south a long block on an expansive avenue, municipal rails down the center, inland again. The restaurant made up half the ground floor of a four-square apartment block not appreciably distinct from any other. He wasn't sure what Nisim meant by *a dive*. Yvo was clean, spacious, busy, though he imagined it would get busier later. "A friend will be joining me," he told the amiable host. "He said you'd know him—Nisim."

The man grinned widely. "Certainly we know Nisim! Little bro's too good to work for his dads but not to eat their cooking." He laughed. "Table for two, then. Nisim's usual is in the garden, if that will suit."

"Sounds lovely." Jafet shook his head. He saw no particular resemblance to Nisim in the man, who was merely handsome. "He didn't tell me Yvo was a family concern."

"It would have *slipped his mind*," Nisim's brother said, leading Jafet farther in to the restaurant, then out through a side door. The table stood within the arc of a raised garden bed, out of ready sight or hearing of other diners, private. "I'll bring you a drink, shall I? While you wait."

Jafet took the seat offered him. The tree that shaded the table and the vines that cumbered it smelled alive, fruitful. "Do you stock Granadas?"

"You like the good stuff."

"I *make* the good stuff. The blood orange, if you've got it, over ice. Sparkling water back."

The man, Nisim's brother, nodded. "Shouldn't be a problem. I'll send it out—and Nisim, when he shows up. Holler if you want anything. I'm easy to catch, Dads named the place after me." He was still grinning, but calculation was chewing on simple friendliness.

Acknowledging the calculation, Jafet grinned

right back. "I'm Jafet, Yvo. But the bottle would tell you that." Nisim was going to get told to turn on the charm.

When Yvo left him, Jafet pulled out the new journal, opened it up. Following the prompts, he input the bases it wanted to establish its position within the aether, its being his, nobody else's. It reacted with gratifying speed—or the old journal, the one buried in the nursery's rubble, had been slow, outdated, or his memory of setting it up was blurred by a decade's wear. He fed it his ID when requested, took the lozenge back, and scribed his password on the display. The journal asked him to speak aloud.

He stared at the display. This had never happened before. "I am in a public place," he said.

Voice verification required to proceed.

"You've been marked."

Jafet slapped the journal's cover shut.

"I saw it when I checked your location." Nisim set his tray on the table: icy bottles, icy glasses, a bowl of salted almonds, a bowl of cured olives, a translucent chillbox of ice cubes. "I'm sorry, I didn't want to say anything on the phone—I didn't know what it meant." He shook his head, pulling out the chair across the table and sitting. "The whole way here I was fighting with my boss, then *his* boss." He grimaced. "I accepted your invitation because I wanted to, Jafet."

"Wait." Jafet stared at his hands and the shimmery grey oblong of the journal on the glass tabletop between them. "Explain this to me— *marked*, what does that mean?" He raised his eyes. Droplets of sweat clung to Nisim's hairline. The stark beauty of his features struck Jafet again, a blow of sorts, unmitigated now by the blinding distraction of his ER coverall. "Something to do with why this is being stubborn? Am I in trouble?"

Nisim pressed his lips together until they turned white. "I don't know what trouble means. Safety and Security is interested in you. That's some kind of trouble, I guess? Your old journal was recovered from the site. Somebody saw something in it that concerned him so he marked you—you wouldn't know, nobody would know, but ER's under S&S authority so I saw it when I looked up your position. I didn't know what it meant so I asked, which was a very stupid thing to do." He looked away. "Although I suppose the surveillance routines would have already noticed me looking you up or calling you…. Jafet, I'm sorry. You offered me sympathy and friendship."

"*Interested*…? Wait. Somebody in the Ministry of Safety and Security thinks I've got some connection to the bombing? That's absurd."

Nisim's hands were trembling. "I certainly hope so."

"Wait." Jafet looked at him, the half-stranger across the table, really looked at him. Nisim was on the edge of hysterics, barely holding it off. He was younger than Jafet had seen before, blinded by competence and Emergency Response yellow. His eyes were tight, there were wrinkles around them and on his brow a man so young shouldn't display. "Nisim. They have no right to do this to you."

"To me?" Nisim's eyes widened. His hands

were still trembling.

Hardly thinking, Jafet reached across the table to take them in his own. "They're presuming on our acquaintance, on your kindness. Safety and Security commandeered you out of ER and assigned you to me—to what they think is *my case*. Tell me I'm wrong."

"I was trying to be friendly—to be responsible, to do my job."

"There is no *case*, Nisim. I wasn't involved. Whoever did it—whoever bombed the nursery—" Jafet tightened his grip on Nisim's hands. "They killed hundreds of men without warning or—or justification. All those orphaned babies! They could have killed me. They were trying to destroy the future. I want them caught and punished. There is no forgiveness." When Nisim winced, Jafet released his hands but didn't know what do with his own. He reached for the frosted bottle on the tray. The liquor within glowed vibrant red-orange. The chill of the glass, striking in through palm and fingertips, made him feel alive. "Nisim. They hurt someone important to me—injured him, widowed him, murdered his new son. I just found that out. There is no forgiveness."

Nisim shook his head. He looked away, though there was nothing to look at. "I'm ... I'm supposed to stick on you like—like Eve's judgment on the X-chromosome. Until somebody bigger than me has time to talk to you."

"Is that how they want it?" Jafet regarded the sad, vulnerable, lovely young man. Surely Safety and Security should be going about their investigation—if that was what it was—more efficiently, more covertly. Surely they should know what they were doing. "My dear, we'll just have to make it as painless as we can. To start with—" he said, pouring blood-orange Granadas over the ice in the first small stemmed glass, "we'll get drunk." The ice crackled, steamed.

8

Molucca-city and offshore, Spice Islands: EJ 303 Melky 36

It was the second day. The only full day: Evren and the band had reservations on the Rabdy hydrofoil to Haven. Teldy morning, after the concert, Jafet had gone to the meat factory as usual, unusual as he felt, but met up with Evren again when his shift ended, and Melky was his day off. They joined the rest of the band for dinner. There was endless innuendo to be fended off even as the boys made it clear they thought it was sweet, he was sweet, *they* were sweet together— and then they all went dancing. The sound artiste at the club programmed "Bo" and "Striped Shirt" into his set—it was unclear whether he was aware

Evren was on the floor. And then, just the two in Evren's hotel bed, there was sex. The second-best sex ever in Jafet's experience (first best had been the night before), for half the night, until neither could get it up again.

Not a problem likely to persist. The light and heat of morning sun through translucent curtains that billowed and bellied in the breeze up from the harbor woke Jafet. He knew where he was. He knew whose arm crooked over his shoulder, whose breath heated his nape, whose fingers were tangled in the chain around his neck. The catch parted and the chain slithered off when he sat up, but Evren didn't wake.

Jafet gazed at the man. It seemed far too early to say *his* man, although really, in his mind, he'd said it all along. Asleep, Evren was not as handsome as awake. He looked vacant, slightly stupid, lips parted and drooling. You could see that his mouth was too small for the long, narrow face, a mouth that looked pinched, ungenerous, until he smiled or sang … leaned in to kiss you, eyes half closed, nostrils flared. The stubble on his chin scraped your own stubble, his breath filled your lungs, the pointed tip of his tongue painted your upper lip, and you could withstand no more: you must sink your own tongue into his mouth, dig your fingers into his buttock and shoulder, clasp his chest so tight to yours there was no telling if it were your heart thumping, or his. Options, choices—there were none.

Except to watch. Watch him sleep, gilded by sunlight, glowing amid tousled, sweat-stained sheets (there were other stains). Careful, Jafet reached to untangle his ID chain from Evren's fingers, but not careful enough. Evren's eyelids trembled. He yawned before waking, before opening knowledgeable brown eyes. Grave, calm, generous, he regarded the face looming above him. "Kiss," he said.

It could have gone further, right away, without any effort except the effort one wanted to expend, but Evren was firm. "I have plans," he said. "Little man."

At the marina below the hotel, he led Jafet onto the white sailboat he'd hired. "Do you know how to sail?" he asked.

"Of course."

"So does the boat, I'm happy to say, so you won't need to."

Coffee and breakfast awaited them in the stern. Jafet was almost not enjoying being led around as if he were a child, but only almost. The boat's AI released its tethers and, under power, deftly maneuvered away from the slip, threaded its way through all the other craft out onto the lagoon's relatively open waters.

"Where are we going?"

Evren stretched and smiled indolently. "Not telling." His toes traced the contour of Jafet's calf. "Why are we still wearing clothes? Strip, I'll anoint you."

Stripping would never not be a good idea in this man's company. Jafet stripped. The boat was on a heading for the break in the reef and the open ocean, he noticed, but then cool mist clouded shoulders and back, skin that was already hot, then Evren's hands were evening it out, smoothing it in, and he wanted to notice nothing else—no other sensation than the palms molding flesh to his bones, the momentary impression of lips when Evren encountered a spot he hadn't kissed yet, at any rate not recently. "You're tall, little man," he remarked at one point, as if congratulating Jafet.

"My dads are both tall."

"Are they handsome?"

"I'm no judge of that."

"Adorable?"

"In their own ways. Not like you."

Evren grunted. "Close your eyes, little man."

Mist on his face. The gentle pads of fingers and thumbs, proving his features, molding them, transmuting them. Did Evren think his big nose handsome? Jafet had always believed it too much, distracting. (Evren's nose wasn't small.) Then the hands moved to his chest, took detours to cover both arms, returned to chest (made his nipples stand up), slid down his belly....

"Chop," warned Evren, and held Jafet's hips before it could stagger him. The faint whine of the turbines deepened as the AI powered them through the passage. Ocean air was somehow saltier than lagoon air. Lines rattled and canvas slapped as the sails ran up. The engines cut out. "My turn," Evren said, releasing Jafet to find his own balance.

"Or mine," said Jafet before he opened his eyes, "depending how you look at it."

"Sophist," said Evren happily, surrendering the applicator. He sprawled on the striped cushions that spanned the stern, open, delectable, on display.

"Have you ever thought," Jafet said, kneeling to his task, "that this shouldn't be necessary?" He began with the feet, first kissing each knee. "I realize the archive is eumelanin poor but the alchemists in Births *could* make us darker, more sun proof."

"You don't like my color?"

"Your color is delicious. I don't like you risking malignant melanomas and carcinomas if I'm not around to do this for you."

"You're paler than me, more at risk."

Comparing the rose-brown of his forearm against the olive-brown of Evren's shin, Jafet muttered, "I'm well aware of that." Forearm hair was thicker than shin hair, though you might think otherwise at a glance, one translucent blond, the other black. "It would be why I think of it, eh?" Up the shin, over the knee, onto the thigh. He massaged the long muscles, sun warm, blood warm. "Three hundred years, not a child has been conceived without them messing around—why don't they mess around more?" Resting his cheek on Evren's thigh, he gazed up.

"They can't excise Eve's judgment from the archive, can't bring women back. That's the only kind of *messing around* the government wants them trying."

"But we could be—"

"Less human?" Evren's grin had nothing of humor about it. "The god botherers think we're dangerously close already."

Jafet shook his head. "Different. Better suited to the only world we have."

"Gills and flippers?"

Jafet smacked Evren's thigh.

"Better suited to a world without women?"

Jafet bent again to his task. "Songs and stories, they're all about love, but how many men ever really know what that means?" He didn't know how to say it. "How it feels. My dad said once, couple years ago, that he hoped I wouldn't be like him and my other dad. That I'd be lucky."

"I hardly ever write about love," Evren said, mock offended. "Do you feel lucky, Jafet? Against my better judgment, I do."

Afraid to look up, Jafet barely spoke aloud: "Do you?"

"What? You don't trust the evidence when it's within your grasp?" Sitting up—the *evidence* bobbed—Evren took Jafet's chin in his hand. "Little man, I am at very grave risk of falling for you."

There was something like lava bubbling in Jafet's belly. He felt ill. He wanted to kiss the lips that offered themselves to his. "Would that be bad?"

"Not as bad as carcinomas or melanomas."

"Sorry." Chastened, Jafet went back to work. He wanted to do more than simply *anoint* the evidence.

Evren turned over onto his belly for Jafet to tend his back. "Do you play an instrument?" he asked, voice muffled.

"No."

"Sing?"

"Loudly. Badly. Why?"

Evren did not reply. Jafet dug his fingers into

wide shoulders, kneaded pliant flesh with his palms. Evren groaned. "I might have tried to get you drafted into the band."

"Evren." Jafet looked up, shocked by the sting in his eyes.

White sails bellied full, steered by its faithful AI, the little sailboat bore down on a small green island. They had been underway scarcely four quarters: when Jafet glanced back he saw they had not gone very far at all, the towers of Molucca-city still rose high above blue waves, the south-easterly islands had not grown appreciably larger. But their goal (it could not be doubted) lay in open sea, as isolated as could reasonably be desired. He knew it would be uninhabited.

"Evren. Evren, you did write that song for me."

"I'd had the tune for a while—" Awkward, Evren pulled his legs out from under Jafet, twisted, sat up. "Ah, no, little man. Jafet. No crying." He wrapped his arms around the taller, younger man. "No, what's this? I went to significant trouble to make you happy, dear little man."

9
Haven-city, Haven-archipelago:
EJ 313 Zizdy/Tanndy 03

Nisim was recalcitrant: he was drunk. Jafet was drunk, too, but he wasn't afraid—just angry. Not angry with lovely Nisim, who kept saying things that made him feel tender. "You don't want to go home," he said, exasperated. "You don't want to go to my hotel. Where do you want to go?"

Clumsy, Nisim detached himself from Jafet's support, stumbled a few steps down the avenue. He carried the Granadas bottle, half empty, possibly not the best idea. Halting, he looked up as though trying to find the tops of the buildings and began to sing.

Five words in—he sang badly, because he was drunk—Jafet recognized the lyrics Evren had written for him ten years before and felt angry, then tender again. It had hardly been Evren's most popular release. "I can't take you there," he said, approaching Nisim carefully. He snagged the bottle from a riskily loose grasp. Nisim was still singing. Every year Evren's crew tried to nudge one of the old recordings into the public consciousness, remind people of the back catalogue (people like Nisim, who would have been eleven possibly when that particular song was released), but the song Nisim sang had never been one of those. He got to the white sail on the horizon, Ziz, Tanin, and Teli in the sky—stopped. Accompanied, fully arranged, the song didn't end so abruptly. Jafet caught him as he staggered.

"How do you know that song?"

"What?" Nisim coughed, several times, but they were just coughs. "I love Evren—I know all his songs. I'm his biggest fan."

"I—" Jafet had long ago forfeited any right to protest. "He's in the hospital, you know."

"They bombed him!" Nisim twisted in Jafet's arm, burrowed into his chest.

"They say he'll recover."

It was late, two or three quarters to midnight. Yvo had thrown them out, essentially, with a look for Jafet that said: You got my baby brother poisonously drunk—now take care of him. Jafet was willing enough—he had no choice, really, if Nisim was to fulfil his assignment, but he chose anyway. He liked Nisim, liked the handsome young man who had told him stories from his job and his draftee travels and jobs over dinner, almost boasting (Nisim had spent half a year in the lemon orchards of Citron-island, just across the sound from Olives and Jafet's distillery), then remembered and became shy. Liked him better (he thought, but he was drunk, not in his right mind) than any man on short acquaintance since meeting Enric on Faraway all those years ago. "Nisim," he said, stroking the young man's hair. "My dear. We can't stand in the street all night."

He steered Nisim down the avenue, toward the mouth of a street that would take them east to the corniche. They were not the only men out this late (probably not the only drunks) but it seemed to be a quiet neighborhood. The white headlamps of an approaching street-rail jitney made him wonder where it might take them—the clubs? They could dance the rest of the night away, sweat out the alcohol.

The mere thought exhausted him. He led Nisim into the narrower, perpendicular street, away from the rails. Nisim was co-operative enough. He stumbled now and then but he was trying. He didn't argue, didn't speak at all. In less than a quarter, they reached the brightly lit corniche.

Any other night, Jafet imagined, there would be crowds. The avenue was far from deserted but every man appeared isolated, preoccupied by his own thoughts and fears, readying himself to go somewhere, do something, but not ready yet. There were no groups, no couples. He drew Nisim out of shadow, onto white pavement. The nearer men seemed to wince.

Away, you felt uneasy indoors because indoors might fall on you without much warning (grand

and petty syzygies were plotted out years in advance, of course, but as bad as those quakes could be they weren't always the most severe). So you made a point of building intelligently, of knowing where doors and vulnerable people were, of conducting much of your life outside away from things that might collapse. The climate wasn't helpful—every three or four winters a hard frost slashed into Olives (north of the bay, and up the Spine, on the other side of the island in the barley- and wheatlands, winters were reliably severe)—but you knew the consequences and dealt.

The archipelagos of the moon were all tectonically stable and lay in the tropics. In Haven, in the Spices, the Australs, the Windwards, it was seldom cool, never cold. Jafet imagined Nisim scarcely knew what a coat was, had of his own choosing worn trousers only once or twice: his sojourn on Citron-island had fallen during spring and summer. Haven's streets and parks might be shaded against Melek's full strength, but for ease and comfort you went (or stayed) indoors, where architecture and urban planning conspired to keep you cool and safe. Unless business called you, you'd avoid the corniche and its tourist throngs— except at night.

It wasn't cool but it wasn't hot. And indoors would not reassure.

Reaching the seawall, Jafet stood with Nisim, one hand on the younger man's shoulder. Their shadows broke on the parapet, then fell ten meters to the sands where they stretched, attenuated, almost to the lapping waters of the lagoon.

Beyond the reef, swells glowed fitfully with internal radiance, but the bioluminescence didn't seem to penetrate the lagoon, its dark water marred only by the faint road of sickle Teli, smallest of the moons. "Let's go down," Jafet suggested.

Nisim didn't reply but he didn't fuss when Jafet urged him toward the stair-head. On the bottom step, Jafet toed off his sandals and almost overbalanced when he bent to retrieve them. Nisim grabbed his arm. "Take off your clothes," he said. He had already dropped his own sarong, shrugged off the bright waistcoat that was more ornament and vehicle for pockets than garment. "I'm going in the water."

"Are you sure?"

"That's why you're coming with me." Almost rough, he grabbed the hem of Jafet's shirt and grappled it over his head. "Come on."

Naked, Nisim started across the sand, not running but walking fast and without much wobble. Jafet stuffed their clothing and the bottle under the stair and hurried after. All qualms aside, he liked the look of Nisim nude, the strong column of his spine, his firm, lean buttocks and long legs. He already knew he found Nisim's soul amenable, his face breathtaking. It might be a complication—a débâcle—a brief delight....

They reached the edge of the lagoon at the same time, feet slapping the film of water that firmed the sand. When it deepened to their ankles, Jafet said, "Please be careful. I'm almost as drunk as you."

"We'll be fine. I have appropriate training."

Jafet wasn't reassured. The water felt nearly as warm as the air, still, calm. It was a long walk to get as deep as his knees but then the descent steepened. Next time he looked, Nisim was swimming away, submerged but for his head, though his hands must surely touch bottom as easily as his feet. Jafet gave in and sank to his knees, struck out after Nisim, mimicking his lazy, old-man's breaststroke. He was surprised, after a few hundredths, five or ten meters, when his feet couldn't find the sand below.

"Refreshing?" Nisim asked.

"Not so much," said Jafet honestly.

Nisim laughed, a pleasant noise, the first time Jafet had heard him laugh. "You grew up on Away, where the ocean's *brisk* and there's no reef to tame the surf. I hated it, the one time I tried. It scared me." He ducked his head under, came up sputtering. "A lot scares me, it would seem," he said less happily.

"Nisim, I think I've figured out what … troubled Safety and Security about my journal."

Ducking under again, Nisim swam a little farther away, two meters or less. Surfacing, he trod water, not looking back. "Not now. Please. Just—not now."

It seemed wise not to reply. Jafet swam closer, then swam beside him when Nisim set out again. After a time, Nisim turned onto his back and simply floated, wallowing in the mild swell. Jafet imitated him. The lamps of the city stained the sky overhead, washed out all but the brightest stars, but Jafet thought he could pick out the tiny orb of Uriel almost directly overhead, straining at its tether. He had visited nearly everywhere in the world but he hadn't climbed the elevator into space. (His vodkas did.) He thought perhaps he didn't need to.

"Jafet, let's go in. I think I'd like more of your vodka, if you'll allow it."

He followed Nisim, taking it slow. Eventually his feet brushed sand again and he rose to walk, striding to catch up. Again he couldn't help but admire Nisim's back, his easy gait, his sleek wet head. He reached to place his palm on Nisim's hip.

Nisim flinched, halted, brushed the hand off, almost violent.

"Oh." It was scarcely a breath, all Jafet could muster, seeing Nisim's expression. In the long run, that made it easier—in the short, not much harder.

10
Uninhabited islet off Molucca-island, Spice Islands:
EJ 303 Melky 36/Rabdy 37

"Listen, Jafet," Evren said, "twelve fivers isn't such a long time."

"Sixty days. Twelve hundred intervals. Forty-eight hundred quarters." It was simple math, he could do it in his head. "One hundred twenty thousand hundredths. It's a long time, Evren. A hundred twenty thousand is a much more appropriate number. Even then, what is it, five shows, ten days? I'll be chasing you all over Away and the attendants. Presuming I can ask for leave. Presuming you'll have time for me."

"Little man." When Evren sat up, Jafet, leaning

on his chest, perforce had to sit up too. "Pour me a drink. Pour yourself one as well—and don't mix them up!" Evren didn't care for vodka, though he'd made sure there was a bottle on the boat for Jafet. He wanted flavor as much as, or more than, effect and drank a dry red wine from the volcanic slopes of Vinland, northwest of Olives. He looked forward, he said, to visiting the vineyards again when the tour brought him to Away in twelve fivers. He'd scheduled a two-day break, though the band wasn't playing Vinland.

Jafet poured the wine. Taking the glass from him, Evren lifted his hand and kissed the back. Not to allow Evren to see how that affected him, Jafet turned away. He pulled the vodka bottle from the chillbox and splashed a little into his own glass. He wasn't so sure he liked vodka himself but it was what Matxin drank and Matxin's son didn't know any better. Evren had made him take a sip of the wine but the smell alone disagreed with him.

The sun had set some while since. Now Ziz hung a few degrees from setting, orange and ponderous above the illuminated towers of Molucca-city across the water, while little Teli, white and chalky as tofu, floated nearly overhead. Tanin was not to be seen, and the boat had furled its sails before grounding itself on the beach in the morning. It wasn't Evren's song: it was life. Jafet leaned forward, propping his chin on one knee. He couldn't tell himself he was unhappy because it would be a lie.

"It's what I do, Jafet—travel, sing, entertain people. If I get famous enough someday, I might

be able to do more of it, most of it, in the aether
… but I don't know that I'd want to. I can't stop
loving my work or earning my living just because
I've maybe met the little man of my dreams."

Have you? Jafet didn't dare ask. Maybe?

"And you, for another two and a half years,
you go where the induction board sends you. No
getting around it. I'm grateful they brought you
here at the right time to find me."

Jafet held his breath. He wanted Evren to
touch him.

"But Jafet, it's too new, it's too soon, we don't
know each other well enough yet to risk—
everything—"

"Have you been in love before?"

Behind him, Evren coughed. It sounded
painful but Jafet hardened his heart. He waited till
Evren's spasms passed and asked again, "Have
you? Because I feel—I'm feeling *so much* that I
don't know what it is. I know it's too soon. I
know we both have responsibilities. I know that.
I'm not as young and stupid as you think. But I—
Evren, I want to crawl inside you. It scares me
how much I want you. How much it's more than
sex. Until last night and today, I didn't know I was
unhappy." He held his breath again, certain with
sick assurance he'd said too much.

The first thing was the arms that grappled him
around the rib cage, forcing him to exhale. "It
scares me, too," was the second thing, and the
third, "I don't think you're stupid. No stupider
than me, anyway. Little man. Little man, I so don't
wish to be parted from you—not even a day, let
alone sixty, not before I know you inside out and

backward and forward, top to toe." Evren kissed his neck, below the ear. The same spot as his first kiss. "That's a long way, you know, top to toe. It might take years."

"More than a hundred twenty thousand hundredths, maybe?"

"I should think quite a lot more." Evren's little laugh was breathy, hot on Jafet's neck. "Jafet, if I could think of any way to keep us together while this is still new, give us more time to discover each other, I'd leap on it so fast—"

"You have commitments."

"Show Zizdy night, six thousand kilometers from here."

"You have to keep the band occupied. I have to watch the meat tanks."

"They liked you, you know. Maybe it shouldn't be, but that's important." Evren laughed again. "Gerrit conceded, but Diogo said he'd sex you up in a hurry if he thought he had a chance. I told him I'd rip his fingers off one by one."

Jafet's turn to snort. "You *need* his fingers. Diogo's attractive, I guess, but too little for me. I'd be afraid of breaking him."

"He's big enough where it counts."

Breaking Evren's hold, Jafet wrestled him to the sand, pinned him down—he was bigger than Evren, too. "Did you just say that?" he demanded.

Evren grinned, breathless. "Jealous?"

"Yes! …No. No—" Confused, Jafet released his hold, laid his head on Evren's chest. "I want you so much, want so much of you, that I don't want to deprive anyone else of you either."

They were silent a while, breathing. Evren

toyed with Jafet's hair. Waves lapped at the sand a few meters away, slapped the hull of the grounded sailboat with a sound like distant, muffled applause.

"When I was around nine," Evren said at length, "my dads.... I think they thought they were like you said your dads are. Best friends who decided to be together because it was better than being alone and they trusted each other to raise kids together. But, you know, they were in *like*, not love, they didn't think love was for them. But then they met Nenad. He started working in Conn's office. Conn liked him so they went out drinking or whatever and sometimes Juste went along too. And then Juste and Nenad were going out more often than the three of them together or Nenad and Conn. And then Nenad moved in with us. It was very confusing for me because my dads were still the same with each other as they'd always been but Juste—he *glowed* when Nenad was around and Nenad got all happy whenever Juste came into the room. Conn and Nenad were just friends. Conn never spent a night in Nenad's room, not that I ever saw, when they kissed it was simple affection. My big brother tried to explain it to me. I don't think he was really old enough to understand it himself. He said the immersives and songs and stories were lies, white lies to make us feel better. Of course, I knew that before the women died it was mostly women and men who fell in love with each other. Only rare, unusual, *special* men ever loved another man like the stories. Or wanted to. It was biology, my brother said, evolution: there were good evolutionary reasons for a few men to be *homosexual* but only a very few. Most of them had to be driven, from deep inside, deeper than conscious thought, to want to make babies with a woman. My brother said that hadn't changed just because the women died. He said our dads always believed they were both like that. They could love each other like friends do, make a commitment to each other, raise sons together, but it was second best, because first best isn't possible. Only Juste found out he was wrong about himself—he could love a man like in a song. It was just that the man he could fall in love with wasn't the man he'd married. But that didn't stop him loving Conn. With a strong, settled, committed, but not passionate love. And Conn, because Juste was his husband and his best friend whose happiness is important to him, he could be happy for Juste. He could share, because what he needed and wanted from Juste wasn't the same as what Nenad needed. They're still together, the three of them. Nenad married them both. Three best friends but only two lovers. They're all my dads and I love them. I don't always understand how they work things out among them but they do. My elder brother and I are Conn's and Juste's sons, but two of my little brothers are Juste's and Nenad's and the littlest one is Nenad's and Conn's."

Evren shifted under Jafet's weight. "You're heavy. Please get off? Not all the way."

"You could get on top of me," Jafet offered.

"No, I'm not finished. Don't tempt me, little man. There's more I want to say."

They negotiated their positions. Because Jafet

was bigger, in the end, Evren settled for reclining in the crook of his arm, both of them half sitting up, with food and their drinks in reach. They'd been a while about it: Ziz, more red than orange, hung behind Molucca's towers like an image on a stage drop. "Are we going back tonight?" Jafet asked.

"I thought we might sleep here and head back early. In time for you to bathe and dress before work."

"Or not sleep?"

"Or not." Evren sipped water, not wine. "When I was nine," he said, "I wasn't as wise or grown up as now. Don't giggle! My brother tried to explain Juste and Nenad to me. I said it wasn't fair. I could see how ... joyful they were. That should be possible for *everybody*, for every man. Didn't they know how, in the nurseries, to make it possible? He thought they did, my brother said, it was partly genetics, partly prenatal hormone levels—he thought they did. Then why didn't they? I demanded. Millions of men doomed to be unhappy, discontent, with drives they couldn't satisfy. What if I, what if he were going to end up like that when we grew up. Broken. Why didn't they *fix* it. We have to be ready, he said, but I don't think he believed it, for women to come back."

11

Haven-city, Haven-archipelago:
EJ 313 Tanndy 03

Jafet had not been able to persuade Nisim he should sleep. If Nisim had ever trusted him, it was apparent he did no longer. Nisim didn't wish to talk either, but it wasn't as though it were an inconvenience that could be talked through, solved. It was sad, it was all sad, Jafet was sad. He sat on the balcony, watching out to sea, and listened to Nisim prowl the room behind him, angry and sad and afraid and drunk—he wouldn't let go of the bottle though Jafet had twice implored him to drink water instead, lots of water. Now and then he stumbled into the lavatory to piss. Once Jafet heard him vomit and he wanted, badly wanted, to go comfort him, but they seemed to have negotiated a contract whose terms he feared to break. Water ran in the lavatory a long time. He could only hope some of it was going down Nisim's throat.

When Nisim stopped making purposeful noises, Jafet waited. After a little, he heard snores and allowed himself to breathe deeply, waiting until the voice that told him he must check on the young man could no longer be ignored.

Nisim had made it to the bed before he passed out. He didn't look comfortable and he'd wake up with a hangover, but there wasn't anything Jafet could do about that. He could only watch over Nisim, try to keep him safe. He turned out most of the lamps, fetched himself a pitcher of water, a glass of pomegranate juice (was it from Matxin and Fadi's orchard?), positioned a chair so he could watch in comfort.

The stupidity with Safety and Security was on his mind, because it had brought Nisim to this pass. Jafet gazed at sleeping, snoring Nisim. The unfortunate young man had got drunk because he was sad and scared, but more to steel himself against the possibility of Jafet's desiring him— then continued drinking to drown his mortification over having rejected that desire. Jafet hadn't seen it, until it was too late for them ever to be friends. After the moment on the beach he had no doubts. Jafet had seen Nisim's horror before. Only twice, but you didn't forget it. You had no warning, because men like Nisim longed for affection and they had a gift for friendship—they always hoped this time, *you*, would be different. *You* would be the impossible man whose person did not inspire crippling, enraging revulsion, the

man they could give in to, not wish to kill
afterward. *You* never came.

The extinction of women was a tragedy, but in
the world as it was constituted three hundred
years later Nisim's life was the tragedy. There
could hardly be more like him than there were
men like Jafet, just a few wholly unsuited as only a
few were wholly suited: one was too many.

It was one of the points of argument in the
New People's Manifesto. Not the only one Jafet
had worked out for himself before encountering
the manifesto and, like the others, stated forcefully
and eloquently. Combined with the accident of his
being in the nursery café when the bomb went off
(his surviving the blast, too, doubtless) and the
history of his queries on Ministry of Births
policies before the last election, the pigeonhole on
his old journal for that seditious document, the
tracks of his search for its origin, would be more
than sufficient to *interest* Safety and Security. Jafet's
own first impulse had been to blame the new
people.

Sadly likely it was only one: one new person. It
ought to be a popular movement.

Jafet continued to gaze at Nisim. Unconscious,
the man could not object. The useless—
undesirable—beauties of face and form were
heartbreaking. The tenderness Jafet felt was not to
be borne. He had almost imagined the possibility
of loving Nisim as well as merely desiring him.

He shifted in his chair, uncomfortable, restless.
None of it was to be borne. He lifted the glass of
pomegranate juice but the smell sickened him. He
was still drunk. Though its sweetness coated his

teeth and tongue, he forced the juice down, then filled the glass with water. The taint of pomegranate remained. He was still in love.

Nine years. He had made himself a life—made himself a man—but years could not salve the wound wrought by a scared, stupid, impatient boy. Alone, lonely, abandoned, ashamed, the nineteen year old five fivers into his third global-service assignment had run like a coward through the canefields, into the scrub outback until—looking back—the only sign of Bougainville was the elevated rail line heading south to Port Sugar. He was crying, he was always crying. He was picked up and then, inevitably, was dropped. Evren had travelled to Terra Australis to celebrate his twenty-fourth birthday with Jafet. Before that, Jafet had travelled to Haven to spend his own birthday with Evren ... and the band, and Evren's bewildering family. Not long before that, the New Year's holiday in Westwind when 303 became 304 and the band played to its biggest audience ever but it mattered most that one man in the crowd was Jafet.

One boy: childish, querulous, insecure.

They had quarreled the night before, their voices meeting in the aether somewhere above the open sea between the Australs and Haven-archipelago. "I'll visit again when I can, little man," Evren said, but *when I can* could not be pinned down. After the quarrel, the boy could not sleep. There was no future before him that wasn't too uncertain for rigid youth to tolerate. He chose. He gazed up to the white, burning subequatorial sky, spoke Evren's name into the aether for the last time, and chose to wound.

It festered, the wound, he picked and worried at the scabs, regarded the putrefaction within with horror, with fascination, with despair. He, the man he had made of that boy, was unworthy of love.

He had never been fool enough to believe he would stop loving Evren but there were other ways he could fool himself. When he learned of Evren's marriage (belatedly—he tried not to keep track), he had wanted to congratulate the grooms (the husband a man named Mehrdad of whom he knew, dared to know, nothing more) but once again let pass the chance for Evren to discover he was yet cared for. Desired. *Required.* Now this, the murder of Mehrdad and his and Evren's son and three hundred fifteen others, presented itself as another opportunity. Jafet couldn't despise himself enough. Their boy, their first boy, could already be growing up. He heard Evren's bitter voice say, My son is dead.

"'Bo,'" he said to the aether, "play Evren's 'Bo.'"

In his first letter, after Jafet persisted in blocking his calls and messages and missives, Evren had written, *You told me long ago it was hearing "Bo" made you believe you might love me.* His handwriting was ragged, as if he seldom practiced. *You didn't understand the words but the words didn't matter, it was my voice, the emotions you heard in my voice. You wouldn't let me tell you what they meant. I thought that was charming, really—I was already half in love with you, you know—and it wasn't as though the lyric was profound. The words* do *matter, Jafet. Not nearly as much as you matter and perhaps in a different way than when I*

*first wanted to tell you. Little man, I won't presume to say
you're hurting yourself as much as me. I can't say how
much you're hurting me, I can't comprehend it. Please.
That's all I can say, truly. Just, please.*

Evren had printed the translation, written his
letter on the back. He'd been correct, Evren. He
often was correct. The lyric was not profound.
What popular-song lyric was? Perhaps the original
words, the Hebrew words, were more evocative, if
you understood them. Don't run away, the singer
said. Don't run away from me. I know you're
afraid—I'm afraid too. We can face anything
together. The translated lyric was not profound,
but the tension between the arrangement's dance
beats, trivial, manipulative, expert, and the
impassioned conviction in Evren's voice was.

Nisim bolted out of sleep shouting. "Bomb!"
he yelled. "Another bomb!"

For an instant Jafet didn't believe him. It's a
nightmare, just a nightmare, he was going to say.

"Parliament-island—Uriel's library ... and the
other nurseries!"

"Stop," Jafet told the aether, and Evren
abruptly ceased singing.

"They haven't blown yet," Nisim said. He
made a noise Jafet couldn't interpret and sank
back on the bed, put his head in his hands.

"Nisim?"

"Global ER/S&S alert," said Nisim, his voice
dull. "Somebody broke, messaged his MP.
Haven's nursery was a mistake. Went off early—
intended to be simultaneous with the others.
Crews searching now." He paused, listening. "For
bombs and conspirators both. Somebody gave up

everything he knew." He paused again, longer. Perhaps the dispatcher was listing off the names.

Jafet's heart still hammered. His grip on the arms of the chair was too tight. His eyes were raw, painful. He felt drying tears tighten the skin of his cheeks.

At last Nisim lifted his head, turned toward Jafet. The hostility in his expression made Jafet's heart pound harder. "You aren't a god-bothering fanatic," he said as if he wished Jafet were. Rising to his feet, he stalked between the foot of the bed and Jafet's chair (his trembling knees), out onto the balcony.

Jafet moved his hands from the chair's arms to his lap and rubbed them together, trying to ease the tension. He felt hollow and sick again. That it was god botherers rather than the new people who seemed to be implicated offered no comfort: he'd already convinced himself. The scope of the plot, the depth of the self-hatred, left him able to focus only on Nisim's hatred. God-botherer insanity, foiled or fulfilled, wouldn't change that. Foiled, would it change anything? Deep where it mattered, he still hated himself.

A quarter year after Evren's first letter—a fiver after his last, which said merely, *I keep loving you, Jaf, keep wanting you, but I can't keep talking to you if you won't listen*—he and the band had released four new recordings into the aether on the same day, more than a year after the previous single song. Evren would know, if he chose to audit the receipts, but Jafet couldn't allow that to prevent him purchasing them. Three he had heard before, live, more than once: a bouncy, jolly dance track called "Head Up," Evren's cover of "Ha'anashim Ha'chadashim" (it still made Jafet nervous and excited), and the lovely little white-sail song—that was its title, he finally learned: "A White Sail." He expected the fourth to be "Little Man," and expected to be saddened beyond recourse.

It wasn't "Little Man" and it scared him sick. The arrangement was thick, guttural, grinding—propulsive. The first time he couldn't take in the words Evren sang, only the hurt and anger that stretched his voice out of its natural register into a space that was terrifying, beautiful. *Listen!* the chorus demanded. *Please listen. Just listen. I only need you to listen!*

More horrible than listening to it on his own, when in private he could hate Evren, hate himself, weep, bite his lips until they bled, was going out in the world and hearing his misery broadcast. Club sound artistes played "Listen" repeatedly. It seemed to be on the playlist at every party his acquaintances and co-workers dragged him to. He didn't hear it in Bougainville's or Port Sugar's markets or stores but it came up in taverns and restaurants—on the ordinarily inoffensive playlist that broadcast through the sugar-thick air of the Bougaineville refinery. Critics who had championed Evren called it a spectacular advance over his earlier work, dauntingly complex and uncompromising in arrangement, universal in emotional appeal. Everyone suddenly knew Evren's name, everybody had loved his music before "Listen" made it popular. A lifetime into its popularity, Jafet boarded a hydrofoil home to Olives before going on to his final posting in the farthest north, the tiny, lonely whiskey island, Faraway. Stodgy, middle-aged Fadi said, "I love this song—it hurts me right here—" and thumped his chest over the heart. It hurt him, he said, but his shoulders were rolling to Gerrit's bass.

"Don't," said Fadi's son, turning away. "Please just shut it off."

"What? Jaf, it's beautiful and—and *thrilling*. Don't you like it?"

"It's me," said Jafet, miserable. He ought to be safe in his father's house. "It's me he wants to listen to him."

"Little love, what is it?"

"Shut if off!" Jafet yelled.

Drifts of pollen-like motes fell to the floor and began silently to decompose when Fadi obeyed. Jafet ground a streak of them to finer powder under his foot. "You wanted me to be one of the lucky ones who could fall in love, Dad. Well, I am." He let his father see his face but stepped away when Fadi reached. "I fell in love with Evren. And he with me. You know 'A White Sail'? He wrote that one for me too. Only I ruined it. There's nothing left."

Intruding on memory, Nisim said, "You're crying."

Jafet bit his tongue—yelped at the pain. "Sorry. Not you." He knuckled his eyes, wincing at that pang, tried to still his heart.

"I wanted to ask if you had anything for a hangover." Slow and careful, Nisim sat on the edge of the bed. Between the dimness of the room and the tears that wouldn't stop, it was hard to interpret his expression. "And apologize."

"Not you, I said," said Jafet, hardly recognizing his own voice. "There should be something in my kit, in the lavatory."

"All right. Thanks." Nisim stood up and went away, but too few hundredths later came back and dropped a hand towel in Jafet's lap. Sitting on the bed again, he sipped at the glass of water he'd brought, didn't say anything.

"Shouldn't you go?"

Nisim moved his head. "Haven't been able to get through to anybody who can release me. Anyway, they've already found and disarmed the bombs at Parliament-island and the Gratitude. There's nothing I could help with."

"I'd like to be alone."

"Oh. Sorry." Nisim stood again.

"It was god botherers?"

Nisim cleared his throat. "I'm supposed to call them the cult of Adam's Judgment, not confuse them with the hundreds of thousands of peaceful, law-abiding ... Mother's Sons."

"Is that what they call themselves? I never bothered to ask."

Nisim took a breath, said, "I'll leave you alone."

"Thanks. Yes." Jafet wiped his eyes with the towel. "Please."

12

Bluehouse and Grand Delta, Away: EJ 303 fivers 41 through 48

His second global-service assignment brought him back to Away but he barely understood the wheatlands as part of the same landmass: the vast, eye-stretching flat valley between the coastal hills and the jagged black peaks of the Spine, endless fields laid in stripes like bolts of fabric: wheat, maize, millet, soy. Oats, barley, and rye were cultivated in chillier country to the north, rice in the far south, although it prospered better in the paddy islands of the Windwards. A little quake woke him the first night: he bolted out of bed and the billet house, significantly faster than his housemates, who weren't native. The quake reminded him of home but didn't make it feel that Bluehouse was *near* home. It was far away. Evren was still in Haven-archipelago, staying with his elder brother, writing, rehearsing, playing small clubs with the band, big theatres with the troupe. "I'm going to stop that soon, I think," he said when he called while Jafet was unpacking.

"I fell for you on stage with the troupe," said Jafet, nostalgic.

"I know. What if somebody else does? Some boy even more lovable than you?"

"You're very cruel, Evren." He wanted to call Evren *big man*, but it would sound stupid.

"Thirty-eight days, Jaf. Diogo can't wait to see you again."

"Diogo can play with himself." Jafet hung his coat in the closet. He hardly needed it—he wore trousers, shoes, a sweater, but midwinter's chill felt refreshing after sultry Molucca.

"Jaf," said Evren. "I'm not *waiting* for you. I know we're thousands of kilometers apart but you're *with* me. Inside me. All the time, little man."

"You—" Jafet sat on the bed he hadn't slept in yet. "That doesn't really make it any easier."

"Judgment, no—no, it doesn't, does it? Every pair of blue eyes, every head of pretty wheat-blond hair, I want it to be my little man and it never is. Branko's all weirded out because I get weird when I look at him."

"Branko doesn't look anything like me," Jafet objected.

"Blond. Blue eyes. If he was abnormally tall and handsome too I'd have to throw him out of the band."

"I— Nobody reminds me of you. Just you."

He swallowed. He wasn't going to cry this time—
he always ended up crying. His first Melky off
after Evren left Molucca, he'd gone to a portrait
studio, in Haven-city Evren did the same, they
talked on the phone while sitting to the
portraitists. Jafet had cried a little, but Evren's
image (he'd hung it first thing, opposite the bed)
grinned and murmured inaudibly and looked
gravely happy by turns. Like any 3D portrait,
though, it wouldn't look you in the eye: you only
saw its somber, beautiful caramel-brown irises on
edge, by stealth.

"We've made it through four fivers, Jaf," said
Evren. "We'll manage the eight to come."

Jafet's station, this assignment, was in the
mezzanine under the roof of Bluehouse Mill,
below a row of clerestories. It made him nervous
to be so high in the event of a quake, but the new
team of draftees spent a good part of their first
day drilling against the emergency that couldn't be
predicted, only expected. Sliding down the escape
pole was terrifying and exhilarating, both.

There was real work for him. From his station,
he learned to guide the great, flexible dry hoses
down into the carriers' hoppers, draw up the mass
of grain, and then scour out the hopper's corners.
It was exacting, if not precisely difficult. Two of
his housemates were running cultivators out in the
fields. He couldn't decide whether to be jealous
until he learned the rota would have him out there
soon enough. The rota also told him Melky would
be his day off, as it had been at the meat factory in
Molucca. At the end of his shift, he asked to speak
to the mill manager.

"You'll have worked, what, not quite eight fivers, and you want a whole damned double-fiver leave?" demanded Asger, a fierce, frightening man for all that he was half a meter shorter than Jafet.

"Yes! I mean, I know I can't have it all. Just—just the days he's playing would be more than wonderful."

"What kind of use to me do you think you'd be the mornings after?" Asger peered up at him, frowning, shrewd and a little sad. "He must be something special. Okay."

Jafet hardly dared believe. "Okay?"

"Two fivers. Eight days leave at half pay, and you work like a machine until then, and a double-fiver *working* at half pay when you're done with this idiocy." Unexpectedly, Asger grinned and offered his hand. "I'm not going to stand in the way of passion, boy, it's too rare. Now thank me kindly and get out of my sight."

Jafet was halfway to the door when Asger said, "Evren, was it? I'll have to look him up."

Bluehouse was nowhere, in the middle of nowhere—rather like Matxin and Fadi's orchards but farther away from *somewhere*: you couldn't walk. At top speed, the on-call rail jitney to Lowcastle took two quarters, one way. Few people bothered except on their days off. It wasn't as though Lowcastle was much of a somewhere. They ate together in the canteen (the chef had wearied of his previous job, at Open Cove in the Windwards, which even Jafet had heard of, so the food was the best he'd ever had), immersed themselves in serials, drank, played games, worked out in the adjacent buildings. One of Jafet's housemates, a youth from Angelico in the Spices who reminded him of his old friend Yehonatan, tried to flirt with him. "I have a boyfriend," Jafet had to say, as kindly as he could (he hadn't used the term before—it thrilled him). They spotted each other in the weight room instead.

Then, somehow, astonishingly, it was the day before. "I'm bored. I hate being trapped on a boat," Evren said, aboard only a short while. "There's nothing to look at but ocean, and it takes so long. You know, on the homeworld there was fast air travel. It would be, what, a few *hours*"—he used the ancient term, which Jafet somehow remembered being significantly shorter than an interval—"Haven to Away instead of a day and a quarter day. Why can't we do that?"

"You can. Charter an aerofoil and be strapped down in a tiny cell with VR goggles for entertainment." Jafet had enjoyed his own sea voyages. "Fast for two days beforehand and endure a catheter for the duration so you won't soil yourself."

"I've always wanted to," said Evren, undismayed. "Ever since I crewed a cargo dirigible on global service. But it's so expensive."

"Evren. There's plenty to do on a big hydrofoil. Read a book. Indulge in a trashy immersive. Find yourself strangers to talk to. Judgment—find yourself a stranger to fuck."

"No."

"I'd hate it but—"

"Little man, no. I'm going crazy because I'm on the way but I'm not there *yet*. With you. That's all."

"Shall I complain for you?"

"It would pass the time. More agreeably than the boys' plans. Pherick and Anand and Gerrit will want to play an endless game of tarot so there'll be the fight of the decade over who'll be their fourth and I'll lose. I always lose. I wrote you another song."

"You did?"

"A real song, not like that silly desert-island thing."

"I love that song."

"Well, only because it was the first. Just the lyrics are yours, anyhow, really, and they were all wish and hope. Now I know you, and myself. This one's better. I'm not certain we're ready to play it but we'll do our best."

"Evren," said Jafet. "Stop trying to make me cry. It's no challenge. Wait till tomorrow."

"I *can't* wait," said Evren simply. "I've waited too long already."

Jafet got up early in the morning. He put in two intervals emptying grain carriers at the mill. On his way to the stairs (he was tempted to use the escape pole), Asger called to him from the open door of his office. "You're not supposed to be here, boy."

"I'm on my way out."

"Your Evren?" Asger shook his head. "He's good. I like his music. Tell him he owes me."

"I will!" Running down the stairs and out of the mill, across the quadrangle and into the billet house. Showered, shaved, dressed, checked to be sure he hadn't left anything out of his bag, and out the door again. Almost kicked the tiffin box with his name on it off the porch: lunch—Asger must have asked Ciriaco to prepare it for him.

The achingly slow jitney to Lowcastle, cutting through the fields. "I'm still bored," said Evren. "I told you I'd be bored."

"Aren't you playing tarot?"

"I cheated. Diogo's stuck with it. I might be a little less bored if I hadn't."

"I'm bored, too." He told Evren about the jitney, the fields ploughing off at right angles, furrowed for spring planting but fallow for the remainder of winter. "But you're almost here."

"You're not planning any syzygies for me, are you? There was a big quake last time—scared me to death."

"When was that? Did anything fall down?"

"*I* fell down, little man," said Evren, stern, on his dignity.

At Lowcastle, Jafet caught the express to Grand Delta, south and east, much faster than the jitney, barrelling down between fallow agricultural land and the broad grey-green slow torrent of the Grand River. He was so excited he fell asleep, then woke, surprised, ate his lunch, and slept again, woke again, mouth furry, when the carriage slowed on its approach to the terminal.

Any other coastal town in Away, the rail terminal would be near the port but Grand Delta was built on the delta's myriad islands and the port, an artificial platform, floated on deep waters offshore. A frail dolmuş, rocking on the swift currents of the town's canals, carried Jafet to the ferry landing where he saw open ocean again; a ferry not much larger than the dolmuş bore him out to the port.

Worried he might be late, he lost himself in the complex, had to ask the aether for direction. Through broad windows in the arrival lounge, he made out the hydrofoil's massive white bow-wave, propagating with alarming velocity across the bay's blue waters, before the vessel itself that rode the wave. Half a kilometer out, the foils submerged and the ship became clumsy, slow, balkily maneuvering its way in to the dock.

Everybody else appeared content to wait indoors, in comfort. Approaching the attendant, Jafet said, "Please? My boyfriend—" and the man smiled kindly, waved him through.

"Jaf! Is that—" Evren coughed in his ear. "It's you. Judgment, I'm crying."

Blinking against his own tears, Jafet strode forward. Little figures crowded the rails of the looming hydrofoil's observation deck, too distant and high to distinguish faces. But that knot of six—five of them were waving. "Evren?"

"You're beautiful, little man, and I love you, and you're *mine*. Never doubt it."

13

Haven-island & Praia Dourada, Haven-archipelago: EJ 313 Tanndy 03 - Tanndy 04

In the morning, early, the first minister made an address. Your phone announced the global alert and you stopped what you were doing, confused, or (like Jafet) jolted out of sleep—it hadn't happened in living memory; the last time would have been during the giga-typhoon of 192 that flattened Emils-port in the Australs, killing fifteen hundred. *Emil* and all its cognates were permanently removed from the list of names fathers might choose for their sons and the island itself rechristened Memory.

"My friends," the first minister began in the tone of any father comforting his sons, "all my friends. Yesterday, 313 Zizdy 03, at 05:77 Haven time, a great crime was committed against our commonwealth. Last night, a greater crime—a crime whose consequences I dare not contemplate—was prevented."

Everybody in the world already knew about the Haven nursery so he spoke of that only shortly, eloquently expressing his speechwriters' horror and apostrophizing the dead. He requested a global day of mourning. The count had risen: three hundred twenty-four. In the background, a choir of trebles and countertenors began to sing the names, a piece of cheap theatre Jafet could only deplore. Effective, though. The first minister spoke also of the forty-two bottles crushed or otherwise rendered unviable and asked the world to recognize the grief of bereaved fathers who would never know their sons. But thousands of bottles, he said, had been rescued and the potential persons within would, in time, join their families.

"We know who did this," the first minister said. Jafet was making coffee—he paused. "We know their full plan was far more devastating: it would have meant the end of men on our world." The speechwriters endeavored not to cast blame on the entire congregation of god botherers. The terms *Mother's Son* and *god botherer* were never pronounced and you were meant to infer the Adam's Judgment cult was an isolate band of deluded, sociopathic crazies, their belief system entirely without context or history. Nevertheless,

Jafet imagined, god botherers across the globe would have been warned to lay low. The Teldy 34 pilgrimage to Jannicke's memorial in Olives was unlikely to happen this year, if ever again. "I would assure you that all the cultists are in custody. They will be tried. Justice will be done and the names of those found guilty permanently erased from the list: no child will ever be asked to share a monster's name.

"We also know why the entire plan was not carried out. The bombs were intended all to explode simultaneously, destroying the infrastructure that allows our sons to be conceived and nurtured, erasing the knowledge that would have permitted us to recreate that technology, and, least of all, crippling the government. One of the cult, for reasons he believed compelling, triggered the Haven nursery bombs early. Another, witnessing the tragedy, comprehended nearly too late the abomination he had involved himself in and acted to prevent its completion."

The first minister paused. Jafet carried his coffee out to the balcony. It was a new day. Only a few degrees above the horizon, Melek was striped by the vertical black ribbon of the elevator, just off center of the disc. Jafet clenched his eyes against the negative afterimage and, blind, sat down. He sipped the coffee. The hotel had provided good beans, well roasted.

"Several years ago," the first minister continued, "an anonymous document appeared in the aether. Many of you will have encountered it. I urge all of you, my friends, to access and read the New People's Manifesto—" shocked, Jafet set the cup down too hard, slopped scalding coffee over his fingers— "and give careful consideration to the questions it raises, the debates it asks to be initiated, its demands. To our shame, we in government knowingly ignored those questions, debates, demands. They are not new, though the Manifesto expresses them, perhaps, more cogently and eloquently than previous attempts. Nor was it only this government that ignored them. They ought to have been addressed three hundred years ago. I pledge to you now: they will be addressed.

"Very few knew the authorship of the New People's Manifesto. Its origin was carefully concealed. The writer himself, of course. A small circle of his friends and associates, those who helped him work out his ideas. His husband and two or three other members of his family. And, to our sorrow and, sadly, to the world's benefit, one clandestine member of the cult of Adam's Judgment, a colleague of the writer, in whose twisted vision the Manifesto promised the final extinction of his ideals, the birth of a new world and the death of his god. This man learned, two days ago, that his idealist colleague was to welcome his first son into the world, yesterday, in the Haven nursery. He chose to trigger the nursery bombs early in order to kill the author of the New People's Manifesto.

"I resist saying one death was more tragic than any of the others. Three hundred twenty-four men and boys lost their lives in the bombing. Each was an individual, each an essential member of and an incalculable loss to our commonwealth. But I ask you all, my friends across the globe, to acknowledge the debt we owe the Manifesto's author, whose unwitting, senseless sacrifice permitted eight thousand two hundred seventy-six babies to be decanted in the world's other nurseries in the few intervals since his death. I ask you to mourn his son, murdered only two quarters after being decanted. I ask you to wish a full recovery and some measure of acceptance, understanding, and peace to his widower, who was gravely injured but somehow survived. They are the first New People. Their names will live.

"Mehrdad, professor of ethics and philosophy at Haven's university."

Jafet started, knocked his cup off the table. Porcelain shattered. He felt splashes of coffee burn his shin, a shard graze his skin.

"Eneko, his baby son.

"Evren, the singer, his husband."

"Evren." It was Evren's voice Jafet had heard in the New People's Manifesto—how had he not seen it? *Ha'anashim Ha'chadashim*, he heard Evren sing: he had named them as well: the New People.

Blinking, Jafet moved his feet, felt the sharp bite of porcelain into his soles. He brushed the fragments aside, rose, stepped to the railing. "Evren," he said again.

"Evren is presently unable to take your call," one of the aether's soothing, passionless voices replied. "Do you wish to leave a message?"

"I didn't mean—" In nine years he had not pronounced Evren's name in the tone that would initiate a call. "How is he? Can he receive visitors?"

A very slightly different voice said, "Evren has

been placed in therapeutic coma. His physicians project revival in ten fivers: your message will not be heard before Tanndy 13. Updates on his condition will be posted to his self-advertisement. Several persons are managing Evren's professional and personal affairs during the period of his indisposition, if you wish to proceed."

"No." Speaking to Evren's fathers or brothers or management team—he couldn't. "Thank you, no." Perhaps Diogo or Gerrit or another member of the band, though doubtless they despised him, but Evren first. He was crying again. Always Evren first.

When he looked south through stinging eyes, down the corniche, he saw the gap in the skyline where the nursery had towered. A barge lay at anchor in the lagoon, taking on rubble. Distinctive as bumblebees in black coveralls and gleaming yellow helmets, men and their machines worked over the site. It was too harsh a reminder. Jafer turned away.

Going inside, he called the resort on Praia Dourada to move up his reservation, called the concierge downstairs to cut short his stay, called the ferry dock for the next departure.

Street rail carried him to the dock. He boarded the ferry, stowed his luggage with the purser, ate more breakfast than he wanted before the vessel cast off. The trip would take up the rest of the morning—the ferry made stops at Elevator-island, Potter, and Tooth before Praia Dourada. Jafet sat on deck and watched the sea roll by, unseeing. He had his phone play Evren's entire catalogue—it was cut short halfway through when the ferry reached Dourada-town.

Debarking at the vivid little port, he called a jitney to bear him south through riotous rainforest, past the three peaks Douradans called mountains though anyone from Away knew what a mountain was. Here the environment was less carefully managed than on Haven-island: the air seemed thicker, hotter, more humid. In the open cabin of the slow jitney, Jafet took off his shirt, hiked the hem of his sarong up over his thighs. The fragrance of his sweat conspired with the scents of vegetation and humus, the quick rushing cleanness of a stream running under the jitney's rails, the bitter breath of salt when the route passed above an isolated beach. The sands of Praia Dourada's beaches were not, in fact, golden. He saw—thought he saw—birds like brilliant enameled brooches, insects like winged gemstones, a half-meter-long lizard stretched out on a branch, its scales crusty, grey-green, like moss on a fallen log. Evren continued to sing, unheard by birds, insects, lizards but *heard*. Jafet might have slept for a time.

At the resort on the southern tip of the island—southernmost point of the archipelago— he was greeted by congenial staff who took his bags, led him to his bungalow, provided a light, brilliantly flavored repast, without requiring him to learn their names. He ate, he bathed, he anointed himself with UV-block, he ventured out to the beach below the bungalow. Other men lay or played on the sands but did not approach him, nor he them, until a resort attendant prompted by discreet tact brought him a tall glass of ice water.

He rested in afternoon sun. His thoughts were not restful but he resisted them. At length, he swam a little in the warm lagoon, then rested again, waiting for the sun to set. As it must, eventually it did, bathing the sea in flame, and he went to dinner.

Returning to his bungalow after, he carried a bottle of aged Faraway single malt, which it amused him to imagine he or Enric might have had a hand in casking: it had been laid down during his final year of global service. He poured a small glass, then rummaged through his bags for stationery. The letter case embossed with Granadas's logo was lost in his satchel in the rubble of Haven's nursery (or in Safety & Security's custody), but he always carried spare writing paper and pens when travelling. He sat at the bungalow worktable but did not activate it, sipped his whiskey. The off-white handmade paper looked distressingly purposeful, split-pomegranate logo printed letterpress in garnet ink. Evren, long ago, had used whatever paper came to hand, but he, Jafet, was who he was.

Evren, he wrote, *You survived. May I say how relieved I am? How difficult—and yet how easy—it is for me to believe we should be in the same building at the very moment men who did not believe in love attempted to destroy all possibility of love. I survived as well, but I have the Away native's quake reflex and survived more easily. If I had known you were in the nursery too, I should not have run away. I regret so much. In this moment, chiefly, I regret the deaths of your son and husband. Although I did not know him, Mehrdad taught me … nearly as much as you have taught me. Eneko deserved to live. Words are insufficient. You need not reply. I do not wish to intrude. I merely* need *to.*

Sealing the letter for dispatch in the morning, he set it aside, drank off the last swallow of whiskey, and went to bed, relieved in a way he could not have explained. He slept easily.

For three days, Jafet made no effort to engage in the life of the resort, taking his meals apart, resting, swimming, sun bathing, listening to Evren's songs, thinking, not thinking. The fourth day was his twenty-eighth birthday. After putting on a facsimile of the man they loved for the men he loved who called—his dads, his grandfathers, uncles, cousins, Yehonatan and Yeho's husband and sons, Enric, others—he was weary by mid-morning.

He took out the new journal. Since the attempt to register it at Yvo in Haven-city, he had not opened it. There was no difficulty now, no nonsense about voice verification, the registration had taken. He had missives queued up but they were all either business or birthday greetings and he left them queued. He looked up, looked out over the beach and lagoon and sea, looked back at the small display in the palm of his hand. For the first time in more than nine years, he asked the aether to show him Evren's self-advertisement.

Two men sat in a nursery decantation room, the one Jafet didn't recognize holding a baby brand new from the bottle, pink and plump. Neither man quite smiled. They did not touch. The caption read: IN LOVING MEMORY OF MEHRDAD AND ENEKO. How long, Jafet wondered, how many hundredths before the bombs had the image been fixed? He brushed it aside, blinking.

A brief text notice on Evren's health was well intended but uninformative. Jafet had learned as much from the aether days before. He brushed that aside as well.

The advertisement proper was far more elaborate than the version Jafet remembered. Making no especial effort to find his bearings, he let impulse guide him until he discovered an area devoted to immersive recordings of Evren's live shows. Excited and worried, Jafet riffled backward through the menu until he found the date and venue: *303 Teldy 48, Grand Delta, Away*. On the point of initiating the recording, he stopped. The journal's display was too small. He knew the resort maintained dedicated immersive spaces of varying sizes, but the full unmediated experience, he feared, would be more than he could bear.

Gathering himself together, he went back to the bungalow. He shut the doors and dimmed the windows. He poured himself a glass of water and one of whiskey. He activated the worktable. He sat. He started the show.

They were so young! On a tenth-size hologram stage above the worktable's glowing surface, tenth-size holograms of Anand and Pherick and Branko, Gerrit and Diogo, Evren played song after song. Jafet swallowed, blinked, wept when Evren first vaulted onto the stage, but by the time the band launched into "Ha'anashim Ha'chadashim" he was dancing with the holographic audience, almost as happy as if it were that long-ago night all over again.

"I wrote this next one for my boyfriend," hologram Evren told the audience—told Jafet—and the recording froze.

"Evren has left you messages, Jafet," the voice from the aether said. "Do you wish to view them?"

"Wait—what?"

A gleaming scroll appeared before him, unrolled. Beginning in 305, for six years, every year Evren had recorded two messages: one on Tanndy 04, Jafet's birthday (today), one on Teldy 10, anniversary of the last time they spoke. In 310, he had recorded a third, final message on New Year's Eve. Nothing in 311 or 312, last year and the year before.

Jafet swallowed whiskey, coughed. "What?" he said again.

"Evren has left you messages, Jafet. Do you wish—"

"Play the last one, please."

He was beautiful. Jafet had never seen anyone, anything so beautiful, naked and alone, huddled on an unfamiliar bed in an unfamiliar room, defenseless. He looked up.

"Jaf," Evren said. "Mehrdad's asked me to marry him. He's giving me no time, he wants to do it tomorrow, he's afraid I'll say no. I haven't said yes, but I won't say no. There's only one lover in all the world I want but I need to understand, I *should* understand by now that you don't seem to want me, and Mehrdad doesn't want any lover at all, only a husband, a companion and friend, a partner in raising sons. I'm already his friend, his companion...."

"Oh, Jaf. Little man. I know you buy my songs—I watch my receipts, you're flagged. When I saw you'd bought 'Listen' all those years ago, that desperate, angry song, I felt sure—but you didn't answer my letters, kept my phone blocked. I thought surely—no, maybe—no, I *hoped* you might come here. Look for *your* song. The first time I sang it for you." Evren blinked, made a small, sad smile. "I've deliberately never recorded it properly. We haven't played it live since that New Year's in Westwind. Remember, little man? Remember how happy we were? How much we—" He looked down, knuckled his eyes.

"I've kept my eye on you, Jaf, as much as I could without being ... unpleasant about it. I'm going to stop that now. It's not fair to you. I wish you continued success and good fortune. I wish you every happiness.

"I'll marry Mehrdad tomorrow. We'll have our sons. But, judgment, Jafet! They should have been *our* sons, yours and mine. I don't—I don't know anymore if you ever loved me as much as you thought you did, or *I* thought you did—I don't understand how you could cut me off for so long—I—" He paused again.

"I don't want to be angry at you. I can't be angry with you. You're inside me, little man, you climbed up inside me and never came out."

14

Olives, Away:
EJ 303 Rabdy - Tanndy 49

They quarrelled once, on the night express to Olives, when Jafet admitted he hadn't told his fathers he was coming, hadn't arranged to introduce Evren to them. "I'm not ready to have the three of you in the same moment," he tried to explain. "To find out I love you better than my dads."

"Not *better*," Evren said, looking away. "Not worse. Not more, not less. Differently."

Jafet was stubborn. "Differently, yes: I never wanted to fuck Fadi or Matxin. But if I had to choose, between them and you—I can't make that decision yet."

"Nobody's asking you to choose, Jaf. *I* won't ever ask you to choose."

"I—I think *I'm* asking."

The lamps in their compartment were dimmed but still wiped the window with glare so Jafet could see the reflection of Evren's three-quarter profile, chin up, eyes half shut, mouth small and uncompromising. There was nothing outside the window, no landscape he'd recognize in dark night or bright sunlight: he didn't know the mountains. The seat vibrated a little, in fast cycles, and there was a hiss at the edge of hearing as the carriage sped along its path of magnetic repulsion and rushing air above the ceramic rail. Olives would be the third concert. He couldn't imagine his fathers would attend. Evren wasn't famous enough (yet) and Jafet had deliberately failed to mark the leave or its occasions on his advertisement—he had never posted any indication he was more than a casual fan. Maybe Yehonatan, if Yeho happened to be home on leave, happened to know Evren's music, but he would be happy for Jafet, no more. Asger had been charming, courtly, after the Glass Falls show—he'd dragooned nearly the whole Bluehouse complement into coming—shrugging off Evren's thanks for allowing Jafet the furlough.

After Olives, Firebeard in the North Attendants. After Firebeard, isolated Blacksands, in the South. After Blacksands ... after Blacksands, a sucking hole he couldn't escape.

"I'm sorry." He reached, trying to escape, touched his palm to Evren's cheek. "I'm selfish."

"*You're* selfish?" A slow, seductive, brilliant grin. "I bought you a ticket. You'll have to cajole another couple days out of Asger—no, sorry, maybe just one? You'll get the regulation three days for New Year's."

"Wait—what?"

Shifting his chin under Jafet's hand, Evren kissed his palm. "New Year's Eve in Westwind. It's a big deal—concert hall, not a dinky little club. I say the promoter's out of his mind but he says he can fill it. Apparently there's an Evren cult in the Windwards I wasn't aware of. I'm coming to get you. Think you can squeeze me into your room at the billet house for a fiver's worth of nights before we go? Judgment, travelling without the band! I can't remember the last time."

"I was decanted in Westwind," Jafet said, unthinking. "…But, Evren, it's a full day between here and the Windwards, at best, not even considering getting from Bluehouse to a port, and no commercial transport on New Year's Eve or Day. It can't be done in four days, not those four, it's at least a fiver."

Evren shook his head. "Your brain works too fast," he said, admiring. "Six intervals, one quarter, maybe better. I chartered an aerofoil. I told you I've always wanted to do that."

"Wait."

"For us, little man. No expense too great, I promise."

"Wait."

"If the experience's too horrible, we'll never do it again."

Evren kissed him for a long time, not long enough for his unease to settle—aerofoils were tiny, fragile machines, smaller and frailer than his dads' catamaran, he couldn't begin to imagine the cost—not nearly long enough.

"Before your mind goes there," Evren said at

last, warm breath gusting on Jafet's throat, "I know it's twenty fivers till New Year's. I know. I counted." His arms were tight, held tight. "I'm sorry. I can't work out any way to get you away from Bluehouse before then. But, Jaf, I promise, anytime I can get a free fiver together, I'll come to you. I can't predict it now, plan it out, but the band can work around *my* needs—chief of them you."

The sucking hole receded a little. Just a little. Jafet knew Evren's tour schedule just as well as he knew the unbreakable term of his own global service. It was his business to know. "I want you all the time, Evren."

"Do you want me *now?*"

Sex was better than it had been in Molucca or on the little island. Jafet wouldn't have believed it possible. Sex in the cramped express compartment (not as cramped as an aerofoil's passenger cell), rushing *away*, astonished him. He couldn't stop laughing.

The new song was almost better than sex. "I wrote this next one for my boyfriend," Evren had said, introducing it at the first show when the applause for "Ha'anashim Ha'chadashim" began to slow. When a small chorus of disappointed groans rose from the front row, he grinned, incandescent in the spotlight—it hurt to look at him. "Sorry, men. I *don't share*." He shaded his eyes against the glare. "Little man, where are you?"

As Jafet made his way to the stage—he'd been threatened with grievous bodily harm—Evren confided, "It's the first time we've played it for him. Global première, right here in Grand Delta.

Historic occasion."

Holding his guitar out of the way, Anand gave Jafet a hand up. "You're going to like this, Jaf," Anand said. "Promise." He swatted Jafet on the rear, urging him toward center stage where Evren waited, impatient. They'd adopted him, Evren's band. Pherick tossed the choicest morsels from his dinner across the table, guffawed when Jafet fumbled the catch, more often than not. Gerrit had dragged him to the local gymnasion that morning, complaining that the others didn't take proper care of themselves and he needed a partner. Even Branko, least demonstrative of the five, most reserved, staring across the room to where Evren was getting silly on red wine, had said, "You do him good. I'm not saying he was unhappy before. Just—you do him good. He wants you. Go."

Evren grabbed Jafet's hand, lifted it high, displaying him. "This is Jafet. Isn't my little man lovely?" There was laughter, some applause, one grumpy call to get on with the music. Jafet felt the blush burning at his cheeks, threatening to crisp his chest hair into curls of char. "I'll tell you, though, it's not just the pretty package."

Without warning, Diogo was picking, a fast, syncopated minor key pattern that repeated and repeated. Evren whirled Jafet around and let him go—he careered toward Anand, who concentrated on his own frets and pick, ornamenting Diogo's line at the same speed, the same rhythm. Just the two guitars, maddening. Nobody had told Jafet what to do. Evren stood near the front of the stage, rocking loosely, waiting. Gerrit, not playing yet, beckoned. Grateful, Jafet retreated to the bassist's side. Evren began to sing.

He sang at the bottom of his register, hoarse and hollow and distorted, laying melody over the repetitive guitars: I'm looking for something. What are you looking for?

I'm looking for something, Gerrit sang (Jafet started), out of step, in counterpoint, his high, true tenor complementing Evren's darker tones. What are you looking for?

I'm looking for something: Pherick next, on the platform behind Jafet, then Diogo, then Branko, then Anand. Jafet had never heard Anand or Branko sing. What are you looking for?

Maybe it's a pomegranate: Evren, up to his normal throaty baritone. Maybe it's a nice loaf of bread, or a nicer glass of wine. No, it's not vodka, I don't like vodka. You don't like wine? That's all right, you can have the vodka. The others kept up the part-singing in the background, the same two lines. Jafet hadn't noticed Gerrit easing syncopated bass in between Diogo and Anand.

Maybe a walk in the streets of the city? Maybe a walk on the beach. Maybe it's a new tune (Branko brought in pizzicato strings, ornamenting Evren's melody, and a hollow percussive drone, fading in and out, that played against guitar and bass lines), though I'm not really tired of the old ones. Maybe it's just sitting here with you, talking about things that don't matter and all the things that do. Maybe that's it.

Pherick stopped singing, tapped the snare in the same intricate, repetitive rhythm as the guitars, and Evren swaggered back from the edge of the stage while the other part-singers dropped out, one by one, till there was only Gerrit's sweet, lonely voice: I'm looking for something. What are you looking for?

Little man (bass drum and hi-hat crashed, Anand and Branko crashed in with heavy chords that nearly drowned out Diogo's picking), I think it's you I'm looking for. Evren grabbed both Jafet's hands. Little man (Diogo and Gerrit sang harmony: Little man), are you looking for me?

Singing, swaggering, Evren drew Jafet to the center of the stage. Little man, I'm happy I found you. Grinning sweetly, he encouraged Jafet to dance with him. Little man, I'm so pleased you found me. Blushing, self conscious, clumsy, Jafet danced. Little man, I'm not going to let you go, we'll go together, wherever you wish. Little man, I'm going to climb up inside you, make myself at home. Little man, it's you and me together, you know that, don't you? Little man—Evren drew Jafet to him, leaned their foreheads together—you know that, don't you? This is the only way it can be. He kissed Jafet's neck, below the ear.

Late at night, in Olives, after they'd exhausted each other all over again and fallen asleep, Jafet spooning Evren, he woke, sat up hard, startled by stillness. "Evren!" Grabbing Evren's shoulders, he shook him. "Evren! Wake up!" Groggy, Evren rolled toward him, smiling dopily. "You have to get out, please, Evren. It's a quake. Out of the building!" The hotel was one storey, every room had an exterior door, he knew where the door was (he always knew where doors were), but Evren heard the word *quake* and panicked.

The earth screamed. Evren screamed. Wrapping his arms around his thrashing man, Jafet picked him up bodily, took a step toward the door. The floor trembled, then jumped. Jafet nearly lost his footing, but if there was one thing he knew how to be scared by it was a quake. Two more savage jolts before he got to the door. At the first hint of a tremor, the hotel's AI had unlocked, unlatched, thrown it wide. He carried Evren over the threshold, dancing with the shaking ground.

Tremors subsided to jittery grumbles in the soil where Jafet set Evren down. He hadn't heard any big crashes and only the expectable startled shouts and shrieks, none of the screaming that meant something was broken, somebody was badly injured, trapped, but it might not be over. "Evren, you're safe. I promise you, you'll be safe here."

"Don't leave me!" Evren was trembling violently, crouched on the ground. It was terror, not chill. He grabbed at Jafet. "Jafet! I'm frightened! You're frightening me! You can't leave me!" The color had drained from his skin. White surrounded his irises.

Calculating, Jafet embraced him again. "Evren, my own, I promise you're safe. The others aren't out yet. They don't know what to do either. They're scared too. I have to go help them. Please, Evren, you're safe." Calculating, he let go.

Whimpering, trembling, Evren buried his head in his arms. "Please come back," he moaned, muffled.

Jafet ran. Hotel staff were leading frightened guests to open ground: Pherick. Gerrit. Anand. Men he didn't know. Branko. "Diogo!" He knew

Diogo's room, never even thought about not being certain where they all were. Found Diogo safe, scared, cowering under the lavatory lintel. "Second safest place you could find, clever fellow," and carried the little man outside. Went back for their precious instruments, the ones he could carry, because he wouldn't forgive himself if he didn't. Went looking for Evren. Found him. Somebody had given him a blanket to wrap around his shoulders, a big mug of hot, fortified coffee to comfort him. "Little man," he said with a tremulous smile, "you came back."

Reached for him, found him, embraced him, let him cry.

Best was reaching and finding Evren there. Always there. Every time. Until he wasn't. Because the big sucking hole got bigger and bigger and swallowed you and you were too afraid to drag Evren in after so you lashed out and told him to *go away*.

15

Granadas Distillers, near Olives, Away: EJ 314 Teldy 01

Jafet sat at his worktable, office door closed. His phone played him "In Memory," the instrumental track Evren's band had released, which attempted (somehow succeeded) to mix a dolorous, frighteningly affecting wordless lament into the peculiar, jittery, dissociated music of "Ha'anashim Ha'chadashim"—everybody knew, now, that Mehrdad had borrowed the translated title for the Manifesto.

New Year's recess over, the trial's final arguments were being heard. Jafet was avoiding them. The conclusion was foregone: the cultists of Adam's Judgment would all be found guilty, would be life-exiled to the deep-sky mines. Before the trial opened, parliament had passed the Birthright Act 313 without serious controversy, deliberately without fanfare. Even the small parties associated with the cowed remnants of the god botherers had the dignity or good sense to refrain from voting. Henceforth, every parent had the right to ask that his son, before conception and during gestation, be nudged toward homosexuality.

Avoiding the trial, Jafet went over the new contract with his deep-sky distributor. It seemed that, in space, the lemon and lime Granadas were preferred over pomegranate or any of the other infusions. It was, perhaps, to be puzzled over, but he wasn't concentrating. His—everybody's—second workday after the holiday, he didn't expect much of himself. Over the music, his phone politely announced a call.

"Enric, I asked not to be disturbed."

"Boss. You've got a visitor." Enric had mostly got over Jafet's gentle refusal to honor their deal of the year before, but still tended to be short. "I think you'd better see him, Jaf. He's in the garden." He disengaged without allowing room for argument.

The four main wings of Granadas Distillers—administration and three stillrooms—enclosed a generous quadrangle, where specimens, those that thrived in Olives's climate, of the trees and shrubs that provided fruit to infuse the vodkas ornamented a pleasant garden. Jafet went out past the empty schoolroom and through the canteen. Standing inside the door, Enric avoided his eye. A few workers—permanent, contract, draftee—sat at tables in the cloister walk with their mid-morning coffee. None was eating or drinking.

None appeared to be watching the trial on their journals, even listening to it. To a man, they stared at the still figure sitting on one of the benches that surrounded the central fountain, black head bent.

Jafet suddenly found it hard to breathe. He believed he had renounced hope. He stepped out of the shadowed arcade, into sun, onto the gravelled walk. The crunch of his footsteps was loud over the sound of the fountain. The seated figure lifted his head a little but didn't turn.

"Little man. I got your letters."

"Evren."

"Sit with me."

Jafet circled the bench, sat, not close enough. Chin up, Evren stared into the fountain's playing waters, did not look at Jafet. His profile had not changed: long straight nose, thin upper lip, the shadow of his beard darker around lips and chin than on the cheek. His hair, cropped short and severe, was densely black—the last image Jafet had memorized, from before the bombs, it had been speckled white. "I've been thinking," Evren said, "of properly recording and releasing 'Little Man.' Finally. I wanted to ask, but you're still blocking my calls."

"Am I? I meant— I'm sorry." Jafet swallowed. "It's your song, Evren."

"If you mean, I wrote it—true enough." Now he smiled, just a little, but still didn't turn. "I wanted to ask regardless."

"I—I would be very pleased. I've often wanted to hear what you'd do with it in the studio."

"You've done well by yourself, Jaf. Impressive establishment, this Granadas. Can we go somewhere else? I—well, it seems I am not merely a famous recording artist and Mehrdad's widower, but the whole world's widower. I give it another year. Meanwhile, it's trying for me, and your people should go back to work." Graceful and supple, he rose to his feet, offered a hand up.

"Of course." Jafet was afraid to take the hand. "Whatever you want."

Evren looked at him for the first time. His mouth was small, severe. "I *want* you to accept my hand and stand up. I *want* to see if you're as tall as I remember, little man."

"I want to be forgiven," said Jafet, miserable.

"We'll negotiate that. I have conditions. I want your employees not to see their boss blubbering. Stand up, Jaf."

Jafet extended his hand. It was grasped—strong, warm. He rose. He still towered fifteen centimeters over Evren, who smiled genuinely, making his mouth generous, said, "I *want* to take a walk. With you. I *want* to see your fathers' orchards. I believe they're not far."

Hand in hand, they turned away from the fountain. At the canteen door, Enric looked troubled, but Ciriaco, standing at the other doorpost, who had seen Evren perform at Glass Falls with the rest of the Bluehouse crew in 303, seen Evren and Jafet in love, beamed. Jafet tried not to see either of them. He held Evren's hand. He wished never to let go.

"I lied a little," Evren said as they entered the passage between Admin and Stillroom 3. "We recorded 'Little Man' a couple of fivers ago. The part-singing was really tough to get down! It came out well, though. I haven't released it generally but—well, go ahead and ask for it. It's encrypted, but not to you."

"Not yet." They emerged from the shadows, walked a few meters into the meadows that surrounded Granadas. "Evren—I'll never stop being sorry for what I did."

Evren jerked his head a little, back toward the distillery. "You did *that* for me, didn't you? All that great enterprise because you thought I might like vodka if I couldn't taste the vodka."

Ashamed, Jafet nodded. "I worked in a distillery at the end of my global service, got interested. But yes, the infusions were for you."

Evren laughed. The sound made Jafet feel faint. "I knew it the first time I saw your name on a bottle. Somebody gave it to me. I regret to report I still don't like vodka, not even yours. Jafet." Evren had stopped walking, held Jafet from continuing. "Little man. A very long time ago, you hurt me very badly. You had your reasons. They weren't valid but they were yours. I think you hurt yourself as badly. All along I knew you were mine. I could let you go—it was hard, I didn't do it gracefully—I could let you go because you were, you *are*, mine. You're inside me. You're the best part of me and the worst part and every part in between. Jaf—" he checked, his expression fierce—"I know you saw my messages, finally. You know what I *want*. I *want* to be yours. I *want* to have been yours for the last ten difficult years but I'll settle for the rest of your life. I'm not offering you a choice."

"I—" He couldn't blink, he had difficulty

catching his breath, his heart was going to batter through his ribs. "I wanted—so many times, so much ... I was afraid and ashamed. I didn't believe you'd have me back." A thick breath sounded like a sob. "I want to cry. I want to call you big man, *my* big man, I always wanted to call you that but you'd think I was stupid." He choked again. "I am stupid."

"I'm afraid you are. I don't mind so much. I'm clever enough, most of the time." Evren wrapped his long arms around Jafet. "Kiss," he said, lifting his chin.

Doubtless Jafet's employees were watching from the windows of Stillroom 3. Some might applaud. Jafet lowered his lips to Evren's. It was like yesterday—yesterday ten years before. It embarrassed him how quickly, how thoroughly excited he got. That wasn't new either, arousal or embarrassment. His tears fell on Evren's face. Evren was laughing into his mouth but pearls of moisture clung to his own lashes.

"Big man," said Jafet wonderingly when they broke apart to breathe, "I don't hate myself as much as I did a moment ago."

"That's good. We'll keep working on it. Come along." He pulled Jafet toward the fringe of the eucalyptus woods. "I'm not feeling like performing for an audience."

They walked through the woods, down toward the sea. Evren said, "I'm not going to feel like performing for an audience for another year or more, you know. I might record studio clips for the aether but ... they don't see *me*. I don't know the man they see. The band's not entirely happy about it but they'll cope. They should just be content I'm alive. Jaf, I meant it about not giving you a choice. Everything I own is in a crate at the port."

"Wait." Jafet stopped short. "What about quakes? You'd do that for me?"

"For me. For us. Maybe a little for you. Anytime in the last ten years. Well, whenever it was you got settled down. I waited. All you had to do was ask. I'm the first new person now and I'm done with waiting."

"Wait. I have to sit down."

Evren watched benignly as he collapsed to the soil, rough with aromatic leaves and peels of bark, leaned back against the trunk of a eucalyptus, looked up. "Big man?"

"Not long," Evren said, grinning. "Your dads expect us for lunch."

"You didn't."

"I'm delighted to tell you I've been conspiring with Fadi for the past half-year."

"You— My dad—"

"I threatened to withhold grandsons if he let you find out."

Jafet grunted. "You wouldn't."

"Well, no, but your father doesn't know me very well. Yet."

"He probably thought I deserved—"

"Jaf." Crouching, Evren took his hands. "I read your letters. I saw you'd visited my advertisement, viewed my messages. Everything was terrible, I'd lost…." Grimacing, he looked away. "By all objective standards, it was far worse than when you … cut me off, though I confess it didn't feel that way. But your letters, Jaf! You loved me! You never stopped loving me! Everything was going to be *right* now. I tried to call. The aether told me, very politely, you had not revoked the block against any and all communication."

"Evren—I'm sorry!" Jafet clutched at retreating hands, but Evren was standing, turning his back, was walking away. "I forgot! Years ago, I forgot it was still in effect. I'll fix it. I'll fix it now!"

"Do that."

It took three hundredths, longer, Jafet thought, than required to institute the block in the first place. When he looked up, Evren had vanished. "Evren! No, please. Where are you?"

"Call from Evren," said the voice from the aether.

"On my way to your dads'," Evren said in his ear. "You can catch up.

"I didn't believe it was deliberate," he continued evenly as Jafet ran through the trees after him, "but it made me angry. I needed time to recuperate, time to shut my life in Haven down and transfer it here—"

"Don't!" cried Jafet, catching up, catching Evren around the shoulders and bowling them both over, rolling them a meter or two across the ground, wrapped in each other's arms. "Don't explain yourself to me." He held the man he loved, kissed him. "Please. I don't deserve it." Kissed him again. "Don't let me hurt you again."

Tousled and breathless, Evren smiled. "Little man, you're bigger and heavier than me and you're hurting me now." But his arms held tight around

Jafet's back, he wouldn't let him up. "It's a good hurt, though." He lifted his chin, raised his lips. "Do you know, we might make them wait a bit longer. I want you, Jaf. Show me you love me. Climb up inside me again."

It was fast, uncomfortable, ludicrous—unprecedented, not to be equalled. After, pulling his clothes back together, flushed, happy, Evren said, "There's worse waiting at your fathers', you know." He stroked Jafet's cheek. "I brought some old friends of yours along. Diogo wants to hug the breath out of you and, I quote, give you a big sloppy kiss and slap you around a little for being such an idiot for such an unconscionably long time. The others weren't so expressive but I believe they look forward to renewing your acquaintance. Over lunch. At your dads'."

"Are *they* moving in with me too?" Jafet felt too relieved, too happy, to be startled. They sat side by side, holding hands. "I'll have to build a bigger house."

"No. Not yet, anyway. Some of them have kids and husbands and whatnot back in Haven. None of them wants to leave the city. I expect they'll be in and out and underfoot like babies, though, from time to time—"

"I like babies."

"Jafet." Evren's hand tightened on Jafet's, painful. "Marry me." He turned his face away. His voice was low, urgent. "I can't lose you too. I can't lose you again."

It was summer—three days after the solstice, fourth day of a new year. Evren had known Away only briefly (the tours without Jafet didn't signify), only in winter. Beyond the eucalyptus woods, meadow grasses were browning off, setting seed. Olives Land Management would initiate the annual controlled burns soon, blackening swaths of hillside and valley with fertile ash, raising fogs of smoke that made clear air precious. In the mornings, sea fogs rolled in from chill sound and bay, seeking dissipation in warm valleys and the sun as it rose over the Spine. In Matxin's plantations, new olives and new pomegranates swelled insensibly toward ripeness; in Jafet's garden, roses and lavender and sky-blue rosemary bloomed, fragrant, intoxicating. Raising Evren to his feet, Jafet held him close. "Happy New Year, big man." He would never let go again. "I've grown up some, I think, while I was being stupid and stubborn and hurting us both more than we ever deserved. Learned a little about caring for, tending what's important—when to hold so tight I can't breathe—" He squeezed. Evren gasped. "When not to demand my own way. You're back, you're mine. I'm yours. We're already married, Evren, if you've forgiven me. We've been married since, I don't know, since the first time you played 'Little Man' for me. Forever. We're already married, but I'll sign the contract, make it official for Revenue and Taxes and all our dads, whenever you want."

Evren's cheek lay on Jafet's chest. "I am," he said, sounding fretful, "more fragile than I may appear."

"As am I, big man."

"We'll probably fight."

"Make-up sex will be terrific. Maybe even as

good as that just now."

Evren snorted. "That was nothing. There are people waiting for us, Jaf."

"Just—" Jafet held him away, gazed into his eyes. "Tell me. I'm not jealous, even if I had the right. He can't be between us, please. Tell me about your husband."

Evren broke from Jafet's grasp, one step. "My other husband. The one I never wanted to write a song for." He didn't sound bitter. He stared up at Jafet. He sounded relieved. "I miss him very much. Mehrdad was my best friend long before I met you. It's a waste and a tragedy. Judgment, I hate them for that." He paused, thinking, then deliberately spat over his shoulder. "They were my ideas, originally, in the Manifesto."

"I wondered, when the first minister told us who wrote it."

"Half an idea or three was yours.... But I wasn't going to write them down or work them out properly—certainly not as well as he did—and although it was all terribly unfair, for me it was abstract: I could love. Did love. Do love. Mehrdad … didn't like to be touched. He broke out in sweats at the thought of sex. I suppose, I hope, he masturbated now and then, but he wouldn't have wanted me to know. I don't remember ever even kissing him."

Jafet thought of Nisim. "I'm sorry. I've known a few people like that."

"He would have divorced me in a flash, happily, if you'd only asked, little man." Evren thought a while longer, squeezing Jafet's hand. "You'll ask, so I'll tell you. I mourn our son. I scarcely knew him, though. I only loved him for an instant, it seemed, before everything blew up. You know I was in an induced coma for a long time, while they made me new eyes, new skin, new hair? I'm still not used to the eyes—colors are the tiniest bit different. My phone fused to the jawbone—they had to grow that new, too. I really am a new person, little man. When they brought me out, I was confused. Then they gave me your letters. Jaf—" again, Evren sounded uncertain— "to me, now, the new me, Eneko, our son ... Mehrdad's son, he's a symbol, like I am for the audience, not a baby, not a person. Not like you."

Jafet held Evren until the weeping ran out. Then they started walking again, together, "Little Man" playing on their phones.

About the author

Alex Jeffers published his first science-fiction story in 1976. Several handsful of stories in several genres have appeared since. His other books are *Safe as Houses*, "a gay novel about family values" (Edmund White), and *Do You Remember Tulum?*, a novella in the form of a love letter. *The Abode of Bliss*, a novel-length sequence of stories set in Istanbul and Boston of the recent past, will be released this summer. He has a number of projects in progress or in mind, including *A Boy's History of the World*, a novel-length return to Rahab which would incorporate "The New People," "Jannicke's Cat" from *M-Brane SF #10*, and "Annie" from *M-Brane SF Quarterly #1*. In his spare time, he designs and copyedits other writers' books. He lives in Rhode Island and at sentenceandparagraph.com.